the world's GREATEST underachiever

HankZIPZER

Hank Zipzer, the World's Greatest
Underachiever series:

The Curtain Went Up, My Trousers Fell Down

Who Ordered This Baby? Definitely Not Me!

The Life of Me (Enter at Your Own Risk)

A Tale of Two Tails

the world's GREATEST underachiever

Hank Z!pZer

WHO ORDERED THIS BABY?
DEFINITELY NOT ME!

HENRY WiNKLER & LiN OLiUER

WALKER
ENTERTAINMENT

First published in Great Britain 2014 by Walker Books Ltd
87 Vauxhall Walk, London SE11 5HJ

First published in the United States as *Hank Zipzer #13: Who Ordered This Baby?
Definitely Not Me!* (2007) by Henry Winkler and Lin Oliver. Published by arrangement
with Grosset & Dunlap™, a division of Penguin Young Readers Group,
a member of Penguin Group (USA) Inc. All rights reserved.

2 4 6 8 10 9 7 5 3

Text © 2007 Henry Winkler and Lin Oliver Productions, Inc
Interior illustrations © 2007 Grosset & Dunlap
Cover by Walker Books Ltd

The right of Henry Winkler and Lin Oliver to be identified as authors of this work has
been asserted by them in accordance with the Copyright, Designs and Patents Act 1988

This book has been typeset in Sabon

Printed and bound in Great Britain by Clays Ltd, St Ives plc

British Library Cataloguing in Publication Data:
a catalogue record for this book is available from the British Library

ISBN 978-1-4063-5576-5

www.walker.co.uk

*To Bonnie Bader, who helps us one word,
one paragraph, one chapter at a time.
And to Stacey always. – H.W.*

*For Henry Winkler – definitely the best
partner ever. Definitely. – L.O.*

CHAPTER 1

"HEY, FRANKIE. MAJOR NEWS," I said into the phone. "We got invited to I Love Chopped Liver Day."

I wasn't prepared for the shriek that came screeching out of the receiver. Frankie Townsend has been my best friend since we were babies, and I'd never heard a sound like that come out of his mouth.

"What's he saying?" my other best friend, Ashley, asked, leaning in close so she could hear.

"He's gagging," I said. "In between the gags, I think he said something about needing to throw up immediately."

"Chopped liver will do that to you." Ashley nodded. "I'll bet he's picturing squishy chicken livers mixed with slimy raw egg and greasy onions."

Suddenly, I felt like I was going to barf, too.

"Could you do me a favour, Ashweena,

and keep the disgusting food descriptions to a minimum?" I asked. I don't know if it was the squishy part or the slimy part or the greasy part, but my stomach was definitely doing backflips.

"Just telling it like it is," she said.

"We're not talking about real chopped liver here, anyway," I whispered to her.

"Tell Frankie, not me," she said.

I waited until the gagging noises had stopped, then spoke.

"Yo, Frankie," I said into the phone. "We're not going to a party honouring an actual chicken's liver. It's honouring Papa Pete's bowling team, the Chopped Livers. They're having their annual Bowl-Off, and they've asked us to do a magic performance."

"That's way better, dude," Frankie said, and immediately switched from gagging to business. Being a very organized kind of guy, he wanted to know the time, place and date they needed us to perform. Being a very disorganized kind of guy, I knew none of the above. Hey, I was excited that I even remembered we were invited in the first place.

"Hold on," I told him. "Papa Pete didn't tell

me the date, but my mum said she wrote it on the calendar."

Ashley and I were standing in my kitchen. Frankie was in his apartment four floors down. He couldn't come up because his mum was making him go through his drawers and take out all the clothes that were too small for him. Frankie is having what you call a growth spurt. Since Ashley and I were having what you call a non-growth spurt, our clothes were fitting just fine, thank you.

Checking the calendar didn't turn out to be so easy. We were talking on the yellow wall phone next to the refrigerator. Our family calendar where my mum had written the date of the party was on the wall way over by the kitchen table. I tried to reach it, but even with the spiral phone cord stretched to its absolute limit, I could only make it halfway there.

"Here, Ashweena," I said, handing the phone to her. "Talk to Frankie while I check out the calendar."

She took the phone and started to talk to Frankie about how much we should charge. Our act, Magik Three, hadn't worked in quite a while, and we were a little out of practice in the charging department. I was pretty sure we'd be out of practice in the magic department, too. Frankie was probably going to pull a courgette out of a hat instead of a bunny.

I went to the calendar and looked for the words "chopped liver". They weren't there. Maybe I had imagined that my grandpa, Papa Pete, had actually asked us to I Love Chopped Liver Day.

No, Hank. That would be too weird, even for you. People don't go around just imagining stuff like I Love Chopped Liver Day.

Then I saw it, written on the calendar in my mum's handwriting, which is messy and hard to read. I think I got that from her. My handwriting is so messy, it looks like the paper has been attacked by a wild herd of dancing caterpillars using all of their legs to write in code.

Chopped Liver Day, as we'll call it, was Monday 8 February. OK, I could remember that, because it was the day after my birthday, which was Sunday 7 February.

I went back to the phone and took it from Ashley.

"OK, Frankie. Write this down. It's Monday night, February the ... uh-oh."

"February the uh-oh doesn't exist," Ashley pointed out.

"I know, I know," I said. "But I forgot the date. I just had it. Where did it go? It was either the day after or the day before my birthday."

It takes four and a half steps to get across my kitchen, and in those itsy-bitsy teensy-weensy steps, the date of the party flew out of my brain, out the window, down ten floors, over to Broadway, got on the 104 bus, went to the Empire State Building, shot up to the hundred and first floor and was probably having a great time, eating a sandwich and looking out over Central Park.

And me, I was left standing in my kitchen having to tell my friends that I had forgotten the date I had just looked at two seconds before. Welcome to Hank Zipzer's brain. Believe me when I tell you it's plenty annoying in here.

I handed the phone back to Ashley and marched myself over to the calendar again. I stared at the date.

Monday 8 February. Remember that, Hank. It's not hard, even for a guy with learning difficulties. Just stand here for a second and let it sink in. OK, now go.

I spun around to return to the phone, but just before I completed my spin, something else on the calendar caught my eye. It was written in red ink, in my mum's handwriting, and filled up the whole square for Wednesday 4 February. It said:

Baby doctor for Lani.

And next to the words was a funny little drawing of a baby's face with its mouth open, looking like it was letting out a gigantic yell.

Thursday 4 February. That's tomorrow.

Why was my mum going to a baby doctor with Lani, Frankie's mum? I mean, they're friends and they hang out together. But why would you take an afternoon off work to go to the baby doctor? If it were me and I were hanging out with a friend, I'd go to the movies or play video games or something.

Then it came to me in a flash!

"Ashley," I whispered. "Tell Frankie we'll call him right back."

"Why? What's wrong?"

"No questions. Just hang up. Now."

"Hey, Frankie," she said. "We'll call you back in a minute. Hank's ... um ... Hank's ... having a ... um ... hunger attack. He needs a piece of cheese or a slice of aubergine or something. Bye."

She hung up the phone.

"Aubergine, Ashweena? Really."

"Hey, don't blame me. I wasn't expecting to have to cover for you. What's wrong with you, anyway?"

"Look at this, Ash. On the calendar. It says *Baby doctor for Lani*. That's Lani, as in Frankie's mum, Lani."

"You don't think..." Ashley's voice trailed off as I watched her start to twirl her ponytail like she does when she's thinking really hard.

"Yes, I do," I answered. "I think Frankie's mum is pregnant. And my mum is going with her to the baby doctor tomorrow."

"Wow, this is big," said Ashley.

"Humongous."

"And weird," said Ashley.

"Extremely."

"Do you think he knows?" she asked.

"He would have said something. A guy can't keep a secret like that from his two best friends."

Ashley sat down at our kitchen table and pushed her glasses back on her nose. She was wearing her blue glasses with the purple rhinestones to match the blue and purple dolphins she had rhinestoned on her tennis shoes. When she finally spoke, she sounded very, very serious.

"Hank, we have to tell him. He's going to need our support."

"Don't you think we should let his mum tell him? I mean, after all, she's the one who's having the baby, not us."

"What if she tells him when we're not here?" Ashley said. She was twirling her ponytail a mile a minute now. "And what if he freaks out? He'll need to talk to us so we can tell him that sure, it's a big change, but he'll probably adjust to it one day."

"You're right," I agreed. "We need to point out to him that babies only cry all the time for two or three years, max. And that spit can usually be washed out of your clothes before it smells really awful and starts to crust."

"It's the least we can do for him," Ashley said.

Ashley picked up the phone and dialled Frankie's number. As soon as it started ringing, she handed me the receiver.

Thanks, Ashley Wong. Save the hard part for me.

"Hello, Frankie," I said, trying to sound

casual. "It's me, Hank Zipzer. Hold on a sec."

Ashley was waving at me like her hands were asleep and she was trying to wake them up.

"Hank, you've got to sound like nothing's wrong," she whispered.

I nodded and went back to the phone.

"Hey, Frankie. Yeah, I'm back... Yeah, I know you know my voice... Yeah, I know we've talked every day since the day you were born. Yeah... I just thought that maybe I should tell you who I was in case I sounded weird or anything... Oh, not that there's any reason to sound weird. I mean, nothing weird is going on. Well, maybe something weird is going on somewhere in the world, but not here in my apartment in New York City. Nope, here everything is just normal, like it always is. Isn't it normal, Ashweena?"

Ashley grabbed the phone out of my hands. Obviously, she couldn't stand it any more.

"Frankie," she said. "Meet us in the club-house right away. We have to talk."

She slammed the phone down and started for the door.

"It's got to be done," she said. "And we're the ones to do it."

This was going to be tough, I thought.

I mean, how do you tell your best friend that his life as he knows it will never be the same again?

CHAPTER 2

As we rode down in the lift, my head was spinning with how to break the news to Frankie. But, truthfully, all I could think of were the millions of ways a new baby could mess up his life for ever and beyond that.

TEN WAYS A NEW BABY
CAN MESS UP A KID'S LIFE

1. You're having a messy sandwich, you reach for a napkin and you grab a used nappy instead.
2. I can't go on with this list. I'm still recovering from Number One. (No pun intended.)

Baby! CHAPTER 3

THERE MUST HAVE BEEN SOMETHING in Ashley's voice that alarmed Frankie, because he was waiting for us at the lift door when it opened on the basement floor.

"What?" he said. "Talk to me."

"I think it's better if we talk in the clubhouse," I said.

"I know that tone of voice, Zip," Frankie said. "It's your 'we got a problemo' voice. The one you used when you messed up and didn't record *The Moth That Ate Toledo* for me. Man, that sucked."

"Haven't I apologized enough for that?"

"Right. I forgive you. So, what's up? What's the problem?"

"Let's go and sit down in the clubhouse," Ashley said.

"Great idea, Ash," I said, a little too quickly. "Let's take a load off."

Ashley and I headed down the hallway, past the laundry room, towards the storage room that we use as our clubhouse. Mrs Fink was in the laundry room, hanging up her gigantic underwear on a wooden rack next to the dryer.

"Hi, Mrs Fink," I called as we turned the corner.

"Hi, children," she called. "If I knew you were coming down here, I would've brought cherry strudel."

"That's OK, Mrs Fink," Frankie called out. "We're not going to be here that long."

"That's what he thinks," Ashley whispered to me. "It's going to take him a while to get over this news."

"After he hears this, he'll wish he had some cherry strudel," I whispered back. "With ice cream on top."

As we rounded the corner and came into the clubhouse, Ashley and I both pointed to the sofa at the same time.

"Have a seat, Frankie," we said together.

"I will not sit until you guys tell me what is going on," he said.

"We're just going to tell you flat out," Ashley said. "Go, Hank. You start."

"Actually, Ash, I was thinking that you'd be the better person to explain the situation."

"But you know, Hank, when it comes to explanations, you're the king."

We had completely stopped paying attention to Frankie. When we turned around to face him, all we saw was his back because he was on his way out the door.

"I can't take this any more," he said on his way out.

Ashley grabbed his left arm, or maybe it was his right – I never get that straight. And I grabbed whichever arm was left. Together, we yanked him back into the clubhouse and onto the purple flowered sofa that had once belonged to Mrs Park on the seventh floor. When he landed, he almost disappeared in the cloud of dust that shot up from the cushion. I had a sneezing fit, which was good because it gave me a chance to get my thoughts together.

"OK, you two," Frankie said. "I've done everything you asked. I hurried down here. I'm sitting. Now spill."

This was the moment. I took a deep breath and put together the most gentle sentence that would break the news the easiest. But what came out of my mouth was:

"Sorry, dude. Your mum's pregnant."

Ashley just stared at me. "I said to tell him," she whispered, "but I didn't mean to *tell* him ... not like that, anyway."

Frankie looked at me like I had just spoken in a mixture of Chinese and Turkish.

"Let's back up here, dude," he said. "My mother is what?"

"Pregnant."

"My mother, Lani Townsend, who lives in my apartment, is what?"

"Pregnant."

"No, dude. You've got the wrong Lani Townsend. My mother has two sons, eleven and thirteen years old. She is not about to have a child who is zero years old."

"It's true," Ashley said. "We know."

"How do you know and why don't I know?"

"Because it's on my kitchen calendar. Right there in red letters. Your mum and my mum are going to the baby doctor tomorrow for your mum's appointment."

Frankie just sat there, stunned, trying to wrap his brain around the idea. I could just imagine what was running through his head.

"I know what you're thinking, dude," I said to him. "That you're going to have to share your room with someone you've never met. That you're going to be ignored. That all the attention is going to the baby. That your parents won't have time for you because a baby needs so much care and energy."

"Actually, I was thinking about if I'm going to have to listen to baby music all day long, because I can't listen to 'Wheels on the Bus' twenty-four-seven. That is completely unacceptable."

"Maybe he'll like the one about the old lady who swallowed a spider," Ashley said cheerfully. "That's got a better beat."

Frankie didn't respond. He wasn't taking the news well. Ashley and I just kind of stood there, waiting for him to say something. Suddenly, he shot up off the sofa and bolted for the door.

"I've got to go and talk to my mum," he said. "This is weird. Why didn't she tell me about the baby?"

"Because parents are weird," I said. "They never do what you're expecting them to do."

"Yeah," Ashley agreed. "Your mum is probably planning to break the news in a surprise way. I'll bet she's planned a fantastic dinner with all your favourite foods."

"Maybe even party hats," I added.

"And then when she brings out the dessert, which would be both lemon meringue pie and your other favourite, butterscotch Angel Delight, each with a candle stuck in them, she'll tell you the exciting news herself."

"Yeah," Frankie said. "This is about as exciting as a screen door in a submarine."

I laughed really hard and loud. Much harder and louder than the situation required. But can you blame me? I was trying to make him feel good.

"And listen, man," I said. "You've got to act surprised when she tells you. Otherwise, we're going to get into trouble for spilling the beans."

Frankie turned and headed for the door. He stopped when his eyes landed on one of the storage shelves that was stacked with old furniture. I followed his eyes to see what he was staring at. It was a white cradle with folded pink blankets inside. I remember that cradle. It was Emily's, and my parents kept it in their room, next to their bed, when she was a baby. Even though I was really little when she was born, I remember hating the fact that she got to sleep in their room, and I had to stay all alone in my big-boy room.

That cradle was definitely the wrong thing for Frankie to see at the wrong time. I had to do something.

"Hey, listen, Frankie, remember you still have us. Ashley and I are right there for you, no matter what."

"Even if you get ignored a little at first, we'll never ignore you," Ashley added.

"Yeah, we're only a phone call away," I added.

"One short lift ride," Ashley said.

"When the baby's puking or pooping or has gas, you can always stay at my house," I said. "My room is your room."

"Thanks, guys," Frankie said. "But I can't talk about this any more. I need time to think."

"It's almost dinner-time, anyway," Ashley said, glancing at her pink rhinestone watch. "Let's all meet down here after homework, say at seven o'clock."

Frankie just nodded and headed for the lift. Ashley and I watched him walk down the hall. He didn't have that Frankie Townsend bounce to his step. As a matter of fact, I had never seen him walk that slowly.

"It'll be OK," Ashley said to me.

"Yeah, in about fifteen years," I answered.

"I'll meet you back down here at seven," Ashley said. "We should bring cupcakes. Do you have any?"

"No."

"Me neither."

"I know," I said. "I'll bring my PSP. His is broken. He can borrow it for as long as he wants."

We headed out of the clubhouse and over to the lift. Boy, I hate to say this, but I was really glad this wasn't happening to me.

CHAPTER 4

WHEN I WENT BACK to my apartment and opened the door, a smile as long as the George Washington Bridge broke out across my face. That's because Papa Pete was there. He's my grandfather, and he's the kind of guy who would make even a warthog who just ate a lemon smile. That's how much fun he is. "Hey, Papa Pete," I said. "I didn't know you were coming for dinner."

"I didn't know, either," he said, giving me a big bear hug. "Until I got a call from your mother telling me to be here promptly at six o'clock. Seems she has some surprise up her sleeve."

"Uh-oh," I said. "I'll bet she's trying out a new recipe on us."

"Your mother and her health-nut recipes are going to help me lose weight," Papa Pete said. "Ever since she took over the Crunchy Pickle, it's like she's turned my deli into a tofu sandwich stand. What was wrong with corned beef on rye with mustard and a pickle?"

"She says fatty meats are hard on your heart," I said.

"Well, tofu is hard on my taste buds," Papa Pete answered with a laugh.

"You're telling me," I said. "Last week, she served flaming tofu beets. We had to put them out with a fire extinguisher."

"Don't tell her, but that's the reason I ate before I came," he whispered. "Tonight she's probably going to serve fried carrot root. Even a starving rabbit wouldn't eat that."

Papa Pete laughed his butt off. I didn't.

"Hey, Hankie, that was a joke. Why aren't you laughing?"

"Sorry, Papa Pete. I was just thinking about Frankie. He's got a major problem going on."

"Did he hurt himself? Break a leg or something?"

"No, worse. His mum's having a baby."

Now it was Papa Pete who broke out into a smile as long as the George Washington Bridge.

"That's wonderful news. A new baby, a new life in the world. It's a blessing, Hankie."

"Sure, unless you're the one who has to give up your room so it can have a place to sleep."

"Aw. That's nothing compared to the joy a baby brings to a family. The whole house will be filled with the wonderful smells of baby powder and strained bananas in a jar."

"Oops, I didn't even think of the smell part. I have to call Frankie to tell him to get a gas mask. At least that'll help him survive until the baby is potty-trained."

"I remember when your mother was born," Papa Pete said. "Her sister, your aunt Maxine, spent the first year trying to bite her every chance she got. She asked me if we could send her back to where she came from and get a puppy instead. And look at them now."

"Papa Pete, they've just had a huge fight because my mum borrowed Aunt Maxine's black sweater and Aunt Maxine thought she saw gravy spots on it."

"And you know this how?"

"Hey, I don't live in a cave. I heard Mum's side of the phone conversation."

"Well, things go on between brothers and sisters, but trust me, Hankie, there's more in the positive column than there is in the negative column."

"Wow, having a new baby around sounds like

a maths problem. Only you can't erase it."

That made Papa Pete laugh. And, I confess, me too. Sometimes I crack myself up, which is a pretty nice feeling.

We were still in the entryway when Emily poked her face in. "Mum says you have to come to the table right NOW."

"Oh, really, did she say it just that way? Like a sourpuss platypus?"

"I don't suppose you know that the Australian platypus swims with its eyes, ears and nostrils shut – the way you walk around every day."

"That's so I don't have to hear, see or smell you," I shot back.

"Whoa, kids," Papa Pete said. "Be nice to each other. You'll see. One day you'll grow up to be best friends."

"I'm sure that's true, Papa Pete," I said. "And that day will be six trillion billion gazillion years from now."

I was satisfied with that comeback and ready to face whatever flaming organic mishmash my mum was about to serve. I turned and headed to the dining-room table, my head held high.

My dad was already seated, and right away, I noticed a funny look on his face. He looked really pleased with himself, like he had just polished off the *New York Times* crossword puzzle in four minutes flat. That's the only thing I know of that makes my dad smile like that. Or if he gets a seven-letter word in Scrabble that uses the letter X or J. Apparently, that gets him all excited, too.

Emily was sitting at her place, with Katherine the ugly iguana on her shoulder.

"Who invited lizard girl to dinner?" I asked.

"Mum says we're having a family dinner," Emily said, "and that includes the scaly members of the family, too."

"Ohhhhh, that's why you're here."

I sat down at my place, and right away our dog, Cheerio, sprinted across the apartment (at least as much as a dachshund can sprint on four of the shortest legs ever invented) and attached himself to my ankle. He hangs out there during meals, hoping for a shred of anything. He is the only one in the family who actually enjoys what my mum serves. He must have been born without taste buds.

"OK, Mum, we're all here!" I yelled to her in the kitchen.

"Coming," she called.

All of a sudden, she backed through the

swinging door from the kitchen into the dining area. She was carrying a tray of something, trying to balance it while she pushed the door open with her bum. I could see bits of colours, and it didn't look like food, but I couldn't tell exactly what it was. When she turned around, my eyes nearly popped out of my head.

There she was, with a huge smile on her face, holding a tray of ... oh my gosh ... party hats.

And if you looked really closely, you could see words printed on the sides, just under the pompoms. And those words said, "Congratulations, it's a baby!"

CHAPTER 5

IT'S JUST LIKE MY MUM to be a really good friend. She's a very considerate person. I mean, when I have a sore throat, she'll actually make chicken noodle soup from scratch, using a real chicken and stuff. Or if someone calls Emily a nerd, which I completely support, my mum will be right there to tell her that they're just jealous of how much she knows about everything.

But in this case, I really thought she was going overboard. I mean, why was our family having a special dinner with party hats and everything to celebrate the fact that Frankie's mum was having a baby?

"Everybody take a hat and put it on," my mum said, handing each of us one of the party hats. "We have something big to celebrate."

"Mum, isn't this going a little far?" I said. "I mean, Frankie's family is celebrating the same thing six floors down."

"Hank, what are you talking about?" my dad asked.

"Well, you know, Dad."

"Maybe I don't know."

"Enough of that, you two. I have an announcement to make. Everyone hold hands."

"Hey, Mum. I draw the line right here. I'm not holding hands with the lizard."

"Katherine doesn't have hands. She has claws."

"My point exactly."

I could tell that Papa Pete was laughing on the inside. His body was bouncing up and down in his chair, even though no sound was coming out of his mouth.

"Would you just take your sister's hand, Hank?" my dad said. "Your mother is waiting with something important to say."

I took Emily's hand on one side and grabbed Papa Pete's on the other.

"The Zipzer family circle is about to get bigger," my mum began.

Her voice cracked when she hit the word bigger and I thought I saw the beginning of tears welling up in her eyes. "I'm sorry, guys. I promised myself I wouldn't cry."

"That's OK, Randi," my dad said. "They're tears of happiness."

Wow. She was really moved by Frankie's mum's baby.

"Hank and Emily, your father and I are so excited to tell you that you're going to be a big brother and a big sister."

"I can take the party hat off now," I said. "I'm already a big brother to her … and I can tell you, it's no party."

"What I'm trying to say, darlings, is that a brand-new baby is joining the Zipzer family."

"What did you do? Send away for one?" I asked.

"Hank, I'm pregnant."

"You and Lani Townsend are both pregnant? That's really weird."

"Lani isn't pregnant, honey. I am."

I just sat there at the table, holding Emily's sweaty hand, trying to get my brain around the words that had just come out of her mouth. It didn't work.

"That can't be, Mum. I read it on the calendar. With my own eyes. Baby doctor for Lani."

"It's *with* Lani, honey. You just read it wrong. Lani is going with me tomorrow."

I continued to sit there, trying to let that sentence open the door and enter my brain. But Papa Pete shot out of his chair like a rocket and raced around the table to my mum. He threw his arms around her, hugged her really hard and lifted her off the ground.

"That's so fantastic, my darling daughter!" Then he reached over with his other hand and started to shake my dad's hand. "Congratulations, Stan. I'm so excited for the both of you."

He turned to me and Emily.

"How about this, kids? How lucky is this baby going to be to have you two as a brother and a sister?"

"I'm going to be the best big sister," Emily said. "I'll paint the baby's toenails ten different colors. And Katherine and I will read the baby books about all the 91,000 species of insects that live in America."

"That will be very stimulating, Emily," my dad said. "I'll bet that will help the baby to get all *A*'s in school."

I'm pretty sure everybody started to talk all at once, but my brain had turned to cream cheese and it sounded like I was hearing all of them through a long tunnel. Their words swirled around in my head. New baby. Smart baby. Share a room. Crib shopping. Nappy bin. No sleep. Bundle of joy.

Bundle of joy? If this baby is going to be a bundle of joy, then who am I?

Slowly, the truth was starting to sink in. Frankie's life wasn't about to change entirely.

Mine was.

CHAPTER 6

I HEADED DOWN for the club-house to meet Frankie and Ashley at seven. Frankie had definitely heard the news from his mum. And from the look on her face, I could tell Ashley knew, too.

They were waiting for me as I walked in.

No one said a word. They just stared at me.

Finally, Frankie broke the silence.

"Hey, dude," he said. "Remember. We're only a phone call away."

Somehow, that had sounded a whole lot better when it was *me* telling *him*.

CHAPTER 7

THE NIGHT AND THE NEXT MORNING, I went about my business as though I had never heard the words "new baby." I did my homework, sort of. I watched television, sort of. I brushed my teeth, sort of. I ate breakfast, actually very well because I was really hungry, having lost my appetite at the dinner table the night before. *You* try eating after your mum gives you the "good news" that you're going to be sharing everything you own with a squealy, throw-uppy, bald, nose-drippy baby.

In class, Ms Adolf's words swirled around my head but never quite made it inside my ears. All I kept thinking about was that my mother was going to the baby doctor and the baby they would be discussing was someone I was going to be related to for the rest of my life. That thought really blocked my brain, so that the only thing I heard for sure was the bell that announced lunch.

It was Thursday, which is fish-fingers day in the hot queue at the cafeteria. In the cold queue, it was cold fish-fingers day. I am not a fan of fish fingers, hot or cold, for two reasons. First of all, I have never seen a fish shaped like a finger. And second of all, what kind of fish actually goes into that finger? And even more importantly, what *parts* of the fish? That has always been a complete mystery to me. But not the kind of mystery that I actually want to solve by taking a bite.

It was definitely push-your-food-around-on-your-plate day, which means that both Frankie and Ashley had to give me a half of a half of their peanut butter and jam sandwiches. And here's my question. Why would Ashley want a banana on her PB-and-J sandwich? But let's face it, when you're the guy mooching the sandwich, beggars can't be choosers. So I ate it with my lips smiling but my taste buds yelling, "What do you think you're doing, Hank?" I wanted to tell the buds to shut *up*, but everyone would have thought I was nuts, talking to my tongue.

"I've made a decision," I said to Frankie and Ashley.

"What is it?" asked Robert Upchurch,

fourth-grade super nerd and occasional boy-friend of Emily Grace Zipzer. "I'm dying to know." It was hard to understand him since his fish fingers filled his mouth like an entire school of guppies.

Robert had wedged himself into our table because he thought we wanted him there, which we really didn't. He's just one of those kids who doesn't get it. I bet you know one like that.

"Really, Robert?" I said. "That's interesting, because I don't remember giving you a ticket to enter my personal space."

Milk started to dribble out of Frankie's nose, because I got him right mid-sip with that zinger. Then Ashley burst out laughing, too, because we all know that seeing milk come out of a guy's nose has got to be one of the funniest things on the earth.

"Oh, look at that," Robert said. "Your milk has found the canal that connects your mouth, your throat and your nose. It's called the passage of the sinus."

This was classic Robert Upchurch. He has a way of inserting his brainful of boring science facts into every conversation and bringing everything to a grinding halt. The other day, when he was at our house playing Scrabble with Emily, he just casually let loose the fact that fingernails grow four times faster than toenails. I mean, what kind of person says a thing like that during a playdate? What kind of person even knows that? Robert Upchurch, that's who.

Robert picked up his fork and took a bite of the fish finger.

"Congratulations about the baby," he said. "Emily told me the good news."

"Maybe it's good news to Emily, but it's not to me."

"I can understand that," Robert said. "I mean, the nappy problem alone poses a difficult environmental issue. Not to mention the odour factor, which actually makes me dizzy."

I really didn't like the way this conversation was going. It was making me dizzy, too.

"Robert, I think if you moved to another table, you would enjoy your fish fingers even more," I suggested. "There's something about being alone with your food that makes the taste really come alive."

"But they're delicious right here," Robert said. "Don't you just love the crunch?"

Two things were clear. One, the nerd wasn't

moving. And two, he would eat a fried shoelace and find it delicious.

"So, Hank," he said, completely unaware that he was unwanted at our table. "Tell us your decision. America wants to know."

He laughed his snorty rhino laugh at his own little joke. And let me emphasize the word "little" here.

"I've decided that the best way to figure this thing out is to experience it for myself," I said.

"Great idea," Robert said. "What thing, exactly?"

"If you would shut up for five seconds, Roberto, you might actually find out," Frankie said, running out of patience with the little guy in the tie. That's right, Robert Upchurch wears a tie to school every day. And I'm not talking about a clip-on.

"Great idea," Robert said. "I'm going to start right now."

"Well, in thinking about this new baby thing, I'm assuming it's going to be terrible," I began, "but I don't really know that for sure. And as Papa Pete always says, don't knock it if you haven't tried it."

"So what, you're going to have a baby yourself?" Ashley said. "This I'd like to see."

Frankie's nose exploded again and milk came shooting out of both nostrils. Poor Frankie, we kept getting him mid-sip. And we literally lost Robert with that one. He laughed so hard, his bony bottom slid right off the bench and we heard his rhino snort coming up from under the table.

"Robert Upchurch, place yourself back on the bench," came a familiar crabby voice from behind me. It was Ms Adolf, on lunch duty. Why could I never escape her?

"I'm sorry, Ms Adolf," Robert said, picking himself up from under the table. "But I just heard the funniest thing."

Ms Adolf turned to me and shot me a look from her beady grey eyes through her grey-rimmed glasses that sat on her greyish nose.

"Henry," she said. "You know I don't approve of humour anywhere in the school building."

"Oh, do I know that, Ms Adolf. And trust me, I don't, either."

"Then why would you spread your silliness here in the dining room?"

I was about to explain that it wasn't me, but I would never tattle on Ashley, ever. So instead

I said, "It just slipped out, Ms Adolf. As if my tongue stepped on a banana peel."

That made Frankie laugh again. But I saw him shoot his fingers up to pinch his nostrils to make sure that no milk would come out in front of Ms Adolf. He stopped the milk just in time.

"Just remember, Henry, that in the dining room we use our tongues only for those activities associated with eating and not for jolly childish remarks."

With that, she turned on her grey heels connected to her grey shoes attached to her grey legs, which were covered by her grey skirt, which were ... well, you get the grey picture. And she stomped off to go and harass Luke Whitman, who was marching around with fish fingers in his ears and two fingers stuck up his nose. That guy has got some big nostrils.

"Where was I?" I asked, which is pretty typical of me. I'm an expert at losing focus. I can lose focus faster than a speeding car.

"You were about to tell us your idea, Zip," Frankie said.

"Right. I've decided that I'm going to get a substitute baby," I said.

"I can loan you one of my old Cabbage Patch

dolls," Ashley said.

"Not a doll," I said. "A living, breathing baby substitute."

"Like a baby iguana," Robert said, who was a reptile fan just like Emily. "Oh, this will be so wonderful for Katherine. I sense her loneliness, sometimes."

"Put a sock in it, Robert. It won't be an iguana, either. I've had enough of reptiles for the rest of my life."

"So what are you going to get, specifically?" Ashley asked.

"And then once you get it, dude, what are you going to do with it?" Frankie added.

"I'm going to take care of it," I said. "I just don't know what the *it* is yet. But I figure whatever it is, I'll find out for myself what it's like to be a big brother to a baby."

"You having a baby, Zipperbutt?"

Oh no, it was Big Ears Nick McKelty. And of all the sentences that large-mouthed bully could have overheard, it had to be the one about me being a big brother to a baby. If there was anyone in the world I didn't want to have that information, it was Nick the Tick. He is the school bully, and has been using me for target practice since

45

kindergarten or even before. I know you know him, because there has got to be a Nick McKelty in your school, too. Maybe he's not tall and blond and thickheaded like this one, but you'll know him by the spit that comes flying out of his mouth when he's insulting you.

"No one said anything about a baby, McKelty," I said. "You must be hearing things. I don't know what you're talking about."

His beefy hand swooped down over my shoulder and grabbed the chocolate cupcake off my tray. In the same arm motion, he brought the cupcake to his face and stuffed the whole thing into his oversized mouth, without even taking the paper wrapper off first.

"I think he's talking about the fact that your mum is going to have a baby," Robert said. For a guy with a little pencil neck, that guy sure had a big mouth.

"Sshhhh, dude," Frankie whispered to him.

But it was too late. Big Ears McKelty had heard the news. He opened up his mouth, showing a pile of soggy chocolate slop that he was grinding the cupcake into.

"The last thing this world needs is another little Zipzer," he laughed, spewing bits of the cupcake wrapper all around the dining room.

And you know what? For the first time ever, I had to agree with McKelty.

CHAPTER 8

I HAD ALREADY ARRANGED for Papa Pete to meet me after school. That worked out really well, because he could take me to the pet shop, where I could start putting my substitute baby plan into action. That made me feel terrific, because when I have a great idea, I want to get going on it right away.

"Hey, Hankie," Papa Pete called out when I came walking out of the front door at three o'clock. "Over here."

Unfortunately, "over here" meant that he was standing by the mural on our school wall, talking with Leland Love, the head of my school. Trust me, you don't really want your head teacher chatting with your family, unless you've just won a big award or you're sure the conversation has nothing to do with you. Unfortunately, in my case, that is never the case. It seems like the big guns at school always have something to say about me, and most of it isn't what you'd call good.

"Mr Love and I were just talking about you," Papa Pete said. "He says he thinks it would do you good to be working with a peer tutor after school."

See what I mean?

"I was just expressing to your grandfather the benefits of good solid peer interaction in the studying process, because without it, there is no peer studying process to interact with," Mr Love said.

If you're worried about why you don't understand this sentence, you can quit worrying. No one in my school ever understands anything Mr Love has to say.

My head whipped round to see how Papa Pete was going to respond to the Leland Love talk-a-thon. I mean, we're used to not understanding him. But Papa Pete is a good listener, and he probably actually cared about understanding both sides of the conversation. We kids gave that up in kindergarten.

"Well, now, Mr Love has made a very interesting and deep observation," Papa Pete said. "So deep that I need some time to let it sink in."

Wow, Papa Pete was good at this adult conversation thing. Maybe that's why everyone likes him.

"So, Hankie," he said, turning to me. "What do you say we discuss the importance of solid study habits over a slice of pepperoni-and-cheese pizza?"

"I like the pizza part," I said.

"And believe me, young man, you'll like the study part, too, once you incorporate it into your routine," Mr Love added.

That's what he thinks. I'm here to tell you otherwise.

Mr Love turned to talk to his next victim, Ryan Shimozato's mum, who looked like she was trying to avoid him. But he was too quick. He took a couple of giant steps over to her, so she couldn't get away, and started flapping his jaw right in her face. Maybe that's why he wears those Velcro sneakers – to sprint after parents who don't happen to have three and a half hours to have a conversation with him. Anyway, although I was sorry for Ryan and his mum, it was a great opportunity for Papa Pete and me to sneak away.

"How about stopping in at Harvey's for that slice I promised you?" Papa Pete said.

"That's a great idea, Papa Pete, but could we please just stop by the pet shop first? Pets for U and Me is right up on Amsterdam Avenue, next door to our library."

"Oh, are you getting a new chew toy for Cheerio?"

"Actually, I have a plan that I really want to put into action. And I need to get something at the pet shop to do it."

"So fill me in."

"Promise you won't laugh?"

"Why would I laugh, Hankie? You have great ideas."

"Well, I'm going to get a baby animal," I explained to him. "And hang out with it for a week or so. Just to give me some practice in being a big brother to a baby."

"What a creative idea," Papa Pete said. "What kind of baby did you have in mind?"

"I'll know it when I see it," I told him.

"Remember you live in an apartment," Papa Pete said. "Which immediately rules out a baby elephant."

"So I guess a baby camel is out of the question, too." I laughed.

"Definitely," said Papa Pete. "You could never

fit that second hump through the door."

We laughed about that for two blocks, which brought us right to the front door of Pets For U and Me.

Just before we walked in, I made a mental list of all the animals inside and which ones would definitely *not* be good candidates for a practice baby.

TEN PETS THAT WOULD DEFINITELY NOT BE GOOD PRACTICE BABIES AND WHY

1. An iguana (because I already have one of those in the house, and that is one more than any eleven-year-old guy should have to hang out with).
2. A goldfish (because I don't want to wear scuba gear and swim around the bottom of a fish tank all day).
3. A turtle (because it takes them an hour and a half to follow you into your room, and who has that kind of time?).
4. A hamster (because it pays no attention to you while it spends all its time running in circles around that stupid wheel).

5. A snake (because who wants to watch it digest a mouse for three days?).

6. A parrot (because if I want to hear a creature talk non-stop all day, I'll go into my sister's room).

7. A gerbil (because the fur on their face—)

"Hankie! Hankie!"

It was Papa Pete's voice, pulling me out of my list-making.

"Come on, you're daydreaming," he said. "I can't stand here in front of the pet shop all day. Are we going in or going home?"

"Oh, thanks, Papa Pete," I said, opening the door. "I guess my mind went on a wild animal safari. Sorry."

Most shops have a bell that goes off when you enter, but Pets for U and Me has a tape of jungle birds and monkeys chattering to welcome you. It's cool because the minute you're inside, you feel like you're out of New York City and into the rain forest of South America.

"How can I help you, Hank?" George, the owner, said. "Are you here for more dog treats for Cheerio?"

"Not today, George. I'm here on non-Cheerio

business," I said.

George had some sawdust on his furry beard because he was cleaning the gerbil cages. I don't mean this in a mean way, but he looks a lot like the gerbils in his shop, without the tail, of course. And his front teeth are shorter, so that saves him from being a total gerbil face.

"That sounds intriguing," George said. "What can I do for you?"

"I'd like to see an animal in a baby size, please," I said.

"And may I ask what for?" George asked.

"It's an experiment," I said.

"Oh, so are you interested in a rat or a mouse? They make great pets."

"No, I'm looking for something that's more like a baby. I'd like it to be annoying and spit up occasionally."

George scratched his beard and a couple of big chunks of the sawdust dropped down to his apron. He didn't notice them there either. He seemed to be deep in thought about my request. I was glad that he didn't laugh at me. That was nice of him. I find that people who are nice to animals are usually nice to kids, too.

"How about a parakeet?" George suggested

at last. "Their chirpiness can be annoying to some people."

"Yeah, but what if it flies away? You don't sell bird leads, do you?"

"No, I've never heard of one. But you could invent the first one," George said.

Papa Pete had wandered off and was over in the reptile section.

"Hankie, look at this," he called out. "It's a baby Katherine."

I walked over to where he was. He was pointing at a little green iguana that, I hate to say, was actually kind of cute.

"No, thanks, Papa Pete. One iguana in the house is one too many." I looked into the case at the little guy. "Sorry, buddy, nothing personal," I added.

Last year, Katherine laid almost fifty eggs in our cable box and all the babies nested in my Mets sweatshirt. I think that experience finished off my interest in having more than one iguana in the house at any one time.

George had followed us over to the reptile section.

"We have a great selection of fish," he said. "They don't spit up, but they do pick up bits of gravel in their mouths and then spit them out again. Would that work for you?"

"No," I said. "I want a baby, and babies don't live in water."

"Baby fish do," he pointed out.

"Yeah, but you can't take them out of the water to play with them. And teaching them to crawl is really hard. And if you overfeed them, they explode."

Now George looked really confused.

"Hankie," Papa Pete said. "You have to tell George something more specific about what you want or we'll be here all day."

"Well," I said. "I'd really like it to be baldish, like a baby."

"I've got it!" George said. "Follow me."

He walked around the fish tanks, past the lizards and snakes, went to the corner of the shop and stopped in front of a few small glass tanks. Inside were the hairiest and biggest spiders I had ever seen.

"These are the tarantulas," George said. "This is Rosa. She's a Mexican red-knee tarantula."

"*Buenas dias*, Rosa," Papa Pete said. And we both cracked up.

Rosa was pretty big as far as spiders go. Her

body was brown with red markings all over her legs. If you looked closely, you could see that she had eight eyes, two on top of her body, and three on each side. Boy, with that many eyes, there'd be no way to sneak up on her.

"Poor Rosa, no one wants her," George said, "so she's been with me for three and a half months."

"No offence to Rosa," I said, "but she's not exactly bald."

"Ah, that's the surprise," George said, his furry face lighting up like the neon lights of Times Square at night. "She's hairy *and* bald at the same time."

He reached into the tank and picked Rosa up.

"Watch out," I said. "She'll bite you."

"Tarantulas are scary looking, but they're actually sweet-tempered and docile," George said. "And did you know, they don't spin a web. They catch their prey by chasing them. Don't you, Rosa girl."

He held her gently in his hand and flipped her over.

Wow, he was right! She had a big bald spot on her stomach.

"Why'd her hair fall out there?" I asked.

"It's part of their defence system," George explained. "When a tarantula is attacked, it rubs its hind legs over its stomach and brushes irritating hairs into its enemy's eyes."

"Now that's what I call a smart spider," Papa Pete said.

"I'll take her," I said. "How much does she cost? I've got three dollars and seventeen cents."

"Unfortunately, she's forty-five dollars," George said. "Mexican red-knee tarantulas don't come cheap."

"Could I rent her for a week?" I asked.

"Sorry, Hank. The animals in my shop aren't for rent."

"Could you excuse us a moment?" Papa Pete said to George. "My grandson and I need to have a pet conversation."

Papa Pete put his hand on my shoulder and led me a couple of feet away.

"I like this idea of yours," Papa Pete said. "There's a lot to be learned about taking care of a person from taking care of a pet."

"Thanks, Papa Pete. I like it, too, but I don't have forty-five dollars."

"But you do have a birthday coming up next

week," he said. "And I've been wondering what to get you for your present. Rosa sounds like a perfect gift. Do you agree?"

"You mean you'd buy her for me?"

"You'd have to take care of her. And not just for a week. But I think there's a lot you could learn from her. Like how to rub your hind legs on your stomach." Papa Pete laughed. He cracks himself up, which is a very fun thing for a pensioner to do.

I looked across the aisle at Rosa in her glass tank. She was walking back and forth, her red knees bouncing along like she was strolling down Amsterdam Avenue. I liked her. But did I like her enough for her to be my little sister?

She was a lot better than Emily in a lot of ways. She wouldn't spew science facts in my direction during dinner. And she wouldn't always point out how her grades were better than mine. And she definitely wouldn't borrow my Mets sweatshirt and not put it back in my third drawer where it belongs.

"Yes, Papa Pete. I want her. And I'll take good care of her."

"OK, you got it," Papa Pete said. "One tarantula, coming right up."

He told George that we'd take her, and got the money out of his old brown leather wallet. While Papa Pete was paying and George was putting together the supplies for Rosa, I leaned down to her tank and took a close look at her. It was time to have my first practice session in being a big brother.

"When I introduce you to the rest of the family," I whispered to her, "I need you to be on your best behaviour. That means no rubbing your hind legs at Dad even though he can be irritating … and no crawling out of your tank during dinner. And absolutely no scaring Cheerio, because he's a scaredy-cat but too embarrassed to admit it."

I'm pretty sure Rosa was listening. At least she stopped walking around and stood very still.

"From now on, it's you and me, Rosa," I said. "And remember, I'm your big brother."

Rosa took a step closer to the glass. I'm not going to say she smiled at me. But I can tell you that she had a very pleasant look on her little spider face. I truly believed we were communicating.

So far, I was feeling pretty good.

I liked being the guy in charge. And for the

first time since I heard the news, I thought that maybe this being a big brother thing was not going to be so hard after all.

CHAPTER 9

Boy, was I wrong.

I mean, what was I thinking? Where did that "not so hard" thought even come from?

Here's how it went. Right in the middle of introducing Rosa to my father, she flicked some of her stomach hair right in his face.

And she didn't even wait for dinner to crawl out of her plastic tank.

No, she made her first appearance the next morning on the breakfast table, when she strolled out from behind the toaster, sending my mum shooting out of her shoes, down the hall, into her bedroom. She locked herself in her bathroom and put a towel under the crack of the door to make sure Rosa didn't come in.

After my mum disappeared, Emily came in for breakfast, wearing Katherine on her shoulder. Old Kathy was just perched up there like always, checking out the breakfast table with her beady eyes to see whether she wanted to flick her tongue at some toast or try to lasso in an orange slice. That's when she spied Rosa, kicking back on a slice of toast.

Her beady eyes got really big, and she started to hiss like a leaky tyre. But Rosa didn't back down an inch.

She started to pulsate up and down on that toast, and even let out a little hiss herself. When Katherine saw that, I thought we were going to have to send Katherine to the Hospital for Freaked-Out Iguanas. She just put her tail between her legs and curled up into a scaly little ball. Oh man, that was fun to see.

And even though I had warned Rosa about not scaring Cheerio, she found it necessary to attach herself to his tail, so when he chased it, he got a good look at her and it scared the daylights out of him.

He kept changing the direction of his circles, but everywhere he went, there she was on his tail. It was like she was on a great old-time roller coaster having her own personal amusement park ride, right in our kitchen.

Before breakfast was even over, I had already made a list of all the many ways having a baby in the house, even if it's a baby tarantula, can totally mess things up.

CHAPTER 10

TEN WAYS BABIES AND BABY TARANTULAS COMPLICATE YOUR LIFE

1. As we have all just witnessed together, they do not follow directions from their big brothers.
2. Even though they have arms and legs (and a tarantula has many of them), they can't use them for anything fun like playing catch or skateboarding.
3. They cause a lot of trouble and don't laugh at any of your jokes.
4. They're always the centre of attention whenever there are a lot of people in the room, even though you're there, too.
5. They can't talk.
6. They don't know one action figure from another.
7. They can't make a snack for you when

you're watching TV and you don't want to get up in the middle of the best part.

8. They can't take a message when someone calls you on the phone and you're in the tub.

9. They can't change the radio station when the DJ is playing an annoying song.

10. So, I ask you, why have them around? Beats me.

CHAPTER 11

THE ONLY GOOD THING about my mum being pregnant that I could tell so far was that she was nauseous a lot of the time. Don't get me wrong, I don't want my mum to feel sick or anything. But when a person is nauseous, that person doesn't like cooking, which, in my mum's case, is excellent news for me. I do not need one more tofu surprise with egg whites and mashed Brussels sprouts. Oh, and I forgot the mung beans that go on top. Nobody needs those.

So dinner that night was a pizza from Harvey's. I had eaten a slice the day before with Papa Pete, but as I like to say, you just can't eat too much pizza. I'm sure you agree.

We gathered around the kitchen table and opened the box from Harvey's. Oh no, what had my mum done? Tell me this wasn't true. That beautiful delicious thin-crust pizza covered with cheese and tomato sauce was covered with ... chunks of broccoli and purple-brownish aubergine. The broccoli was buried deep in the cheese, and the aubergine had already slimed and spread all over the pizza so you couldn't even pull it off. My mum looked so pleased until she shot a glance over to me. She could tell by the way I was staring at this alien pizza that the vegetarian delight wouldn't have been my first choice.

"Mum, pizza is not something we play around with," I said. "It's meant to hold cheese, which is meant to hold pepperoni and sausage and meatballs and mushrooms, and maybe an occasional olive. Not broccoli."

"Now, it's a balanced meal, honey," she said. "You've got your grains, your proteins, your fats, and now, your fruits and vegetables. The surprise is that under each piece of aubergine I asked them to hide a piece of pineapple."

No wonder she was nauseous. Now the whole family was going to join her.

We all sat down at the kitchen table wondering who was going to be brave enough to take the first bite. We didn't have to wonder long. Katherine, who was draped around Emily's neck like a winter scarf, shot her long grey sticky tongue out to its full length and snatched a chunk of broccoli right off the pizza. It must have been hot, because instead of putting the broccoli in her mouth, she flipped it in the air and started waving her tongue above her head like a lasso. Suddenly, that pizza was looking pretty good to me. In fact, it was becoming my hero. Anything that can send Katherine into a tizzy is OK in my book.

I had brought Rosa to the table in her little plastic tank. My mum objected at first. But I explained to her that Rosa was there to help me to practise for the new baby, and we certainly weren't going to leave the baby in another room when we had dinner. So she agreed to let Rosa stay, as long as she didn't have to sit next to her.

Anyway, maybe it was the iguana tongue-waving event that caused Rosa to flip out, but all of a sudden, she had crawled out from under her rock, scurried up the side of the tank and was hanging upside down on the top of the tank's lid, pulsating like a giant clam.

"Hey, Emily, get your iguana to get her tongue under control," I said. "She's getting Rosa all shook up."

"Oh my goodness, Hank, you promised you'd keep that creepy-crawly creature away from me!"

my mum said, bolting across the kitchen to the door so she could leave at any moment.

"You've got to get used to her, Mum. She's part of the family."

"It's just something about spiders that I can't even think about," my mum said. "I can't handle all those legs."

"Don't say it so loudly, Mum. You're hurting her feelings."

"I wish Papa Pete had checked with us before buying you a spider. It's a big decision to bring a living thing into the family and it should've been a group decision."

"Uh-huh," I said. "That's exactly how I feel."

"About what?" my dad asked.

"No one asked me if I wanted a baby brother or sister."

"Of course you want one, honey," my mum said. "Think of all the fun you'll have."

"Right. Being ignored by you guys because you're busy changing nappies and teaching it the alphabet."

"Don't be ridiculous, Hank," my dad said. "No one's going to ignore you."

"Except me," Emily chimed in. "But then again, I already do."

"OK, Dad, so when you're on your twentieth round of playing peekaboo, where are you going to find the time to watch the Mets game with me?"

"Maybe the baby will be a baseball fan," my mum said.

"Oh, I hope not," Emily said. "I'm going to teach the baby all about how sound waves affect the insects that live in Central Park."

"Great, we're going to have the first baby in history to run away from home at the age of three and a half months," I said.

"Hank, you're going down the wrong path here," my dad said. "All change is hard, but you're being overly dramatic. Nothing is going to be taken away from you. You're going to get everything you got before and more!"

If what my father was saying was true, then this was the perfect moment to bring up plans for my birthday.

"OK, then let's start with my birthday party," I said. "Last year's was so much fun, I'd like to do it again. Remember, you took all my friends bowling at McKelty's Rock 'N' Bowl, then we had cheeseburgers and hot dogs and played video games. And for my birthday cake, I want that yellow one with chocolate icing from Babka's Bakery."

My mum looked at my dad with a worried expression on her face. That face said "things have changed" to me. As a matter of fact, it yelled it.

"About your party, Hank," my dad said. "We were thinking of something different this year. Fun, but quieter."

"'Quiet' and 'birthday party' are two words that do not go together in the same sentence, Dad."

"Hear me out, Hank. Since your birthday is Sunday, and it's a school night, we were thinking of a nice dinner at home and then maybe a Scrabble challenge."

"Hello, Dad. It's Hank Zipzer's birthday. As in he-can't-spell-pretty-much-anything-but-his-name."

"OK, it doesn't have to be Scrabble," my dad said. "We can play charades. That's always a fun indoor game. Frankie and Ashley will love it. They can come, too, of course."

"Dad, nothing personal," I said, "but I think your body has been officially invaded by aliens who are whispering weird thoughts in your ear."

"I think it sounds like a very stimulating and challenging party," Emily said.

"Oops, those are two more words that should never be in the same sentence with birthday party."

"It's important to keep an open mind, honey," my mum said. "About your party and about the new baby."

"If it's OK with you guys, I think I'm going to go to my room and try to open my mind there."

"Would you like to take a slice of pizza with you, dear?" my mum asked.

"No thanks, Mum. I think Rosa is getting dizzy from the aubergine fumes."

I picked up Rosa's tank and turned to go. I wanted to be in my room, to think things over. It all seemed different. I mean, it wasn't like my parents to plan such a lame birthday party. The only thing I could think of was that their thoughts and attention were on someone else. And I think you and I both know who that someone else was. That's right, the nappy pooper.

As I turned to go, Katherine shot her tongue out in Rosa's direction. Not being an expert on iguana feelings, I couldn't tell for sure, but I'm pretty positive it wasn't a "welcome to the family" gesture. In fact, I think it was more of a "hey, hairy girl, I was here first" kind of tongue flick.

I hate to say it, but I could understand how Katherine felt. I was here first, too. And now my birthday party was getting shoved aside by the new President of the Future Nappy Poopers of America.

CHAPTER 12

As I STOMPED INTO MY ROOM, I used my foot to slam the door behind me ... hard. I wanted them to know that this was not OK with me. I mean, you don't just tell someone they're going to have the worst birthday party of their whole life and then go on with dinner like nothing happened.

"This sucks, this sucks, this sucks," I yelled, making sure to stand really close to the door so everyone in my apartment could hear. Probably everyone in the whole apartment building could hear.

I waited for someone to come in. Maybe my mum with a comforting word. Maybe my dad with a new plan for my party. But no one came. It was me and Rosa, alone in my room. Wow, if I ever needed proof that I had suddenly dropped to number three on the list of Zipzer kids, there it was. It hit me in the face like a wet noodle. Outside my door, they were knee-deep in pizza, having a great old time. And no one cared to even come in and check on how sucky things were for me.

"So this is how it is, Rosa," I said, putting her little tank down on my desk. "It's you and me."

She climbed out from under her rock and scampered up the side of the tank facing me. As I looked at her rubbing one hairy little leg against the other, an idea hit me.

"Who needs them?" I said to her. "I'll give myself my own birthday party."

Call me crazy, but I think she understood.

"Rosa, would you like to come?"

Rosa rubbed one leg against the other again, and I took that as a yes.

OK, I was feeling better. Let them go and have that baby and be all distracted and everything. I could make myself a perfectly fine party.

"So, Rosa, what kind of party should I throw? And don't say anything that has to do with Spider-Man. I've outgrown that. My Spidey tighty whiteys don't even fit any more."

Rosa just sat there on the side of the tank. I could tell she wasn't going to be much help in the party planning department.

"OK, then, I'll call Ashley," I said. "She's an

organizational specialist."

I opened the door to my room and sneaked out quietly. I could hear that the pizza fest was still going on. I crept down the hall to my parents' room, being careful to avoid certain floorboards that I knew creaked. After ten years of creeping down your own hall, you learn these things about your apartment. Like if you ever come to my apartment for a sleepover, don't expect to hop in the bathtub right away, because it takes a long time for the hot water to make its way up the pipe from the basement to the tenth floor. Sometimes it takes so long for the water to heat up, I have to have a snack while I'm waiting.

I got to my parents' room and tiptoed over to the phone by the side of their bed. I dialled Ashley's number.

"Hey, Ashweena," I whispered. "It's me."

"Why are you whispering, Hank?" she asked.

"Good question. I don't know."

"OK, so you're in a weird mood. What's up?"

"I'm throwing myself a birthday party," I said. "And it's very V.I.P."

"What's it going to be?" Ashley asked.

"Good question. I don't know."

"OK, when is it going to be?"

"Another good question. I don't know. But can you come?"

"Good question," she giggled. "I don't know."

"OK, my birthday's Sunday," I said. "How's that sound to you?"

"Oh, I'm so sorry, Hank," Ashley said. "I would love to come, but I have a plan this Sunday. Frankie and I are doing something."

"On my birthday? What could you possibly do that is more important than my birthday?"

"Um ... well ... this is supposed to be a surprise, so don't say anything to your mum ... but we're driving out to New Jersey to a baby outlet where we're going to get a pushchair that converts into a car seat that converts into a playpen that converts into a crib. It's a present for the new baby."

For the baby! Oh man, this new baby was everywhere.

"Fine," I said into the phone. "Have a really great time. Don't worry about it, because I am perfectly capable of having an amazing birthday party that will make your socks roll up and down."

"Hank, don't be mad."

"I'm not mad, Ashley. I'm independent. And don't worry. I'll let you know how great my party was."

I hung up the phone a little too hard. I stomped back to my room, not worrying about the creaks coming from the floorboards. Let them all hear me. Let them all know I am Hank Zipzer, independent party giver and birthday celebrator. King of the Party Hat. Prince of Cake.

Take that, new baby.

CHAPTER 13

I WAS DETERMINED to make this the best birthday party ever, even if Rosa was going to be the only guest. As a matter of fact, this party was going to be so great that once the word got out, every kid in America would want one just like it.

There was no decision to be made. It was going to be at Harvey's, my favourite pizza place at the end of my block on Broadway. I'd have pepperoni pizza and maybe a few slices of yellow cake with chocolate frosting. OK, make that one slice of cake. I'm still working out the dessert part. I'd fill Harvey's with shiny silver Happy Birthday balloons. Oh, and maybe there'd be one silver balloon tied to my chair. And best of all, there'd be presents covering the counter, stacked so high you wouldn't even be able to see Harvey taking the pizzas out of the oven. Well, on second thought, since I was going to be raiding my own piggy bank to buy my presents, and knowing that there was only four dollars and thirty-five cents inside, I'm sure one present would do just fine.

Let's see. Should I get a pink high-bounce ball or a remote-controlled mini racer or—

"Henry!" a voice said. "Would you please inform the class about the three types of cloud formations?"

"A Nerf boomerang," I said, before I could stop the words from coming out of my mouth. I was so deep in my birthday party plans, I had completely lost focus and forgotten that I was actually sitting at my desk in class and Ms Adolf was conducting a lesson in science vocabulary.

"Excuse me, Henry. Why are you speaking such gibberish? A boomerang, nerfy or otherwise, has no place in a science discussion."

"I once heard that if you threw a boomerang hard enough into a cloud, you could create rain," I said, trying to come up with some way to cover my wandering brain.

"Once again, Zipperbutt proves himself to be Mr Stupid." Nick McKelty laughed, spitting bits of graham cracker into the back of my head. Trust me, you don't want to have the seat in front of McKelty, especially when he's sneaking graham cracker treats from a bag he hides in his book for free-reading time.

"At least I'm not a food cannon," I said to McKelty. "By the way, you still have bits of marshmallow stuck up your nose."

He didn't, but I sure had fun saying it.

McKelty grabbed his pencil and used the rubber as a shovel to try to dig out the made-up bits of marshmallow. It didn't matter that the marshmallow wasn't there. It was great just watching him go for them and hearing the class crack up into hysterics.

"Pupils, you know I don't appreciate laughter, especially in class," Ms Adolf said. "School is no place for fun. Now, are you ready to answer the question, Henry?"

"I really am, Ms Adolf. I am totally, one hundred per cent ready. The answer is on the tip of my tongue. If I could just remember the question, the answer would come flying out of my mouth."

"For the life of me, I don't understand why you don't remember the question. What could possibly be more important than the subject at hand?"

"If you really want to know, Ms Adolf, I was thinking about my birthday and making plans for a really special party."

When I said the "really special party" part, I turned to Ashley and shot the words right to her. I wanted her to know that I was completely capable of having a fine time all by myself. Then I turned to Frankie, who sits on the other side of me.

"It's going to involve pizza and balloons and possibly yellow cake with chocolate frosting," I whispered to him. "You know, the kind of cake that's your favourite, too."

"Hey, dude, I feel really bad about your party," Frankie whispered. "Not being able to come and all."

"Hey, don't worry about it. Besides, I can't talk to you now. Ms Adolf and I are having a very interesting conversation about clouds."

"Are you two quite finished with your idle chitchat?" Ms Adolf boomed, tapping her grey shoe on the floor in a definitely irritated way.

Wow, look at that. She has a plaster on her heel. And even that is grey. I have never seen a grey plaster before. I've seen Spider-Man plasters. And *Star Wars* plasters. And fluorescent Snoopy plasters. But I've never seen a grey one. Maybe she paints them.

"Henry, if you don't want an extra homework

packet as a birthday present from me, I suggest you pay attention. Now."

"Right, Ms Adolf. My brain is all yours. Fill her up."

I tried to listen, but my thoughts had other plans. They were back at Harvey's, smelling that sizzling pepperoni, putting up birthday streamers, buying paper hats and horns, and filling that silver balloon with helium.

When the lunch bell finally rang, and I headed out the door, Frankie and Ashley caught up with me in the hall.

"Hey, Zip," Frankie said. "You know I wouldn't miss your b-day unless it was something majorly important."

"Like shopping for a baby you don't even know," I said. "That's majorly important, for sure."

"Our mums are making us do it," Ashley said. "They said it's important that we celebrate the announcement."

"Yeah, well, let me make my own announcement to you," I said. "I, Hank Zipzer, am going to have the most sensational party known to mankind and cumulus clouds, for that matter."

"Who you inviting, dude?"

"I have one friend who's not on baby patrol. She happens to have eight legs, but then, that's all the more of her to enjoy."

"The spider?" Ashley said.

"Excuse me, she has a name. Which happens to be Rosa. And for your information, she knows how to get down at a party."

"Dude, you have lost your mind," Frankie said.

"Correction. It's everyone else around here who has lost their mind over this baby coming. No one even remembers what's important any more."

"Like your birthday?" Ashley said.

"Funny you should mention it. That's exactly what I'm talking about."

"You're really taking this hard, aren't you, dude?" Frankie said.

"I don't think so," I said. "Everyone should do exactly what they want to do. My parents want to have that nappy captain and spend all their time powdering its bottom, good for them. You guys want to hang out at a warehouse in New Jersey, be my guest. Now if you'll excuse me, I'm going to finish planning my birthday bash-zip-ola."

I turned round and walked the other way. I think it was the first time since kindergarten that I wasn't having lunch with Frankie and Ashley.

That baby wasn't even born yet, and it was screwing up everything ... even lunch period. What was next? Break?

CHAPTER 14

"HEY, ZIP," Frankie said after school that day. "Can you meet me in my apartment at four?"

"Why?" I asked him. "What are you going to do, throw me a party?"

"Have you forgotten, dude? I love chopped liver," Frankie said.

"No, you don't. As a matter of fact, last time we had it, you said it looks like the stuff that collects between your toes."

"No, Zip. It's your grandfather's bowling team celebration on Monday. Remember? 8 February. And we're—"

"Oh right, doing magic. I forgot. What trick are you going to do?"

"I don't know. Maybe the biting-the-quarter-in-half trick. Or possibly pulling Cheerio out of my top hat. But I haven't done that in a really long time, which is why we need to rehearse this afternoon."

"Well, Frankie, I'm afraid you're going to have to start without me. I'm going to be a little late. But you can pick up Cheerio. I don't think he has a playdate."

"Where are you going to be?"

"I got stuff to do."

"Stuff, as in?"

"Balloons and hats. Cool party favours. That kind of stuff. I'd get you some, but, oh right, you're going to be in New Jersey."

We had reached the corner of 78th and Amsterdam Avenue. To get to our apartment, Frankie was going to continue straight down 78th for another half a block. Me, I was planning to take a right up Amsterdam. I was heading for the 99-cent store. Now that I'm in the fifth grade, I'm allowed to walk home by myself because our apartment is only two blocks away. Technically, walking home doesn't really include the 99-cent store, but the shop is within the two-block limit, even though it's in another direction. So I made the decision that I wasn't really breaking the rules, I was just bending them a little. Well, I really wasn't bending them, I was twisting them. Maybe not even a twist. Maybe a tweak. Yeah, I was tweaking the rules. Surely my parents couldn't be angry about that. A bend I understand, but a tweak? Come on.

"So I'll see you in a little while, then?" Frankie said.

"Whenever."

"Not whenever, Zip. Get there as soon as you can. Or did you forget that you are my all-important assistant? If you don't hand me the quarter, I can't bite it in half."

"Ashley can do it."

"She's our business manager, Hank. Between you and me, she doesn't have your dramatic flare. You're the best assistant a magician could ask for, dude."

He must've felt really bad for flaking out on my party, because now he was really buttering me up. He used so much butter that I felt like I was sliding down the pavement.

Frankie headed home and I turned right up Amsterdam Avenue. I passed the Silver Star Cafe, where people were sitting sipping coffee in the window. I saw Mrs Fink. She must have been stirring her coffee, because she waved to me with her spoon still in her hand. I wondered if she'd like to come to my party.

Hank, get ahold of yourself. She'd make you

dance the cha-cha and eat her cherry strudel.

When I reached the 99-cent store, I went in and found the birthday party section. It was full of paper plates and cups and party hats and noisemakers and little bags of toys that would make fun party favours.

"May I help you?" an assistant said. She was a tall woman with a big smile and a badge that said her name. In case you're interested, it was Vivian.

"Well, ma'am…"

"Call me Vivian, honey. Everyone does."

"Well, Vivian, I'm throwing myself a birthday party, and I notice that all these supplies seem to be in packs of eight. My party is a little bit smaller than that."

"How many are coming, honey?"

"I believe that would be one and a half."

"A half?"

"I'm the one, and my tarantula is the half."

"You're inviting a spider to your party?"

"As a matter of fact, she's the guest of honour. And pretty excited about it."

"So none of your other friends are coming?"

"Funny you should ask. They're actually going to be in New Jersey that day, so I figured, I can entertain myself and have a great party without them."

"Good for you," Vivian said, giving me a big smile. "You sound like a very independent and resourceful kid."

Well, finally, here was someone who appreciated me.

"So, I couldn't help but notice that you don't seem to have any hats small enough to fit a large spider," I said.

"To tell you the truth, you're the first kid I've ever met who's made that request," Vivian said. "Let's see what else you need."

Vivian was really nice. We picked out a pack of blue party hats and a silver balloon. They were out of the Happy Birthday balloons, but I really wanted a silver one, so I picked one that said, "Get Well Soon." Why not? Everyone wants to be well. The only other silver balloon they had said, "Welcome New Baby," and you can understand why that one stayed in the shop.

The good thing about having a party for one is that you can get a party favour you really want. None of those paddles with elastic string and bouncy rubber balls that break the first time you use them, sending the ball shooting across the room. No mini Rubik's cube on a key ring. I once turned that thing for a month and never got even one colour all solid. No little bags of jelly beans where once you throw out all the purple ones that taste like the way my mum's perfume smells, you're left with mostly banana-flavoured ones, which are even worse because there's nothing banana about them.

I picked the large-size whoopee cushion, which never fails to crack me up. And for Rosa, I picked a rubbery slimy spider that sticks when you throw it against the wall. Not only that, it glows in the dark. I thought she'd get a kick out of that.

When it came time to pay, Vivian was really, really nice. She gave me a twenty-per-cent discount.

"Anyone who throws himself his own birthday party deserves a gift," she said. And the discount was her gift to me.

I have no idea how much twenty per cent of five dollars and fifty-three cents is. But let me put it this way. I handed her a five-dollar bill and I got some change. I have no idea how much change I got back. I can't do that kind of maths in my head. But if you wait until I get home,

I can let you know.

When I left the shop, I was feeling pretty darn good. The plans were in action. The supplies were bought. The guest list was short and sweet. And the only thing left to do was to party like a madman.

CHAPTER 15

THE NEXT DAY was Saturday, a perfect day for a birthday party. I know, I know. My actual birthday wasn't until Sunday, but as I told myself when I woke up, I am an independent party planner, party giver and partygoer, and I can throw myself a party any old day I want. Besides, all the party supplies were sitting on the table next to my bed, staring me in the face, and I just couldn't wait any more.

Oh yeah. Also I had nothing to do that day.

So I got up and went to my drawer and took out the brand-new grey hooded Mets sweatshirt Papa Pete had bought me that I had been saving for the most special occasion I could think of. And to tell you the truth, I couldn't think of a more special one than today. I put that sucker on, and party time shot through my body. The bounce in my step as I headed to the kitchen for breakfast made me look like the happiest guy in the world. I had to remind myself the entire way from my room to the kitchen not to eat too much for breakfast, so I had room for what was coming.

"Hi, honey," my mum said when I walked through the kitchen door. She was sitting at the table, sipping elderberry tea and reading a book. "Don't you look nice today. What's the occasion?"

"Well, I have a few special plans for today," I said, pouring myself a glass of orange juice.

"That's nice. What do you think of the name Ralph? And there was another one... Where is it now...? Ah, Digman... Would that be too unusual?"

There that baby was again, splashing around in my glass of orange juice. Suddenly, I didn't want it any more. In fact, I didn't even want to be at the breakfast table any more. I had completely lost my appetite.

"I'll see you later, Mum," I said.

"But you didn't eat anything."

"I'm saving my appetite for Harvey's," I said. "I'm planning on going there for lunch, if that's OK."

That got her attention. She put down the

baby-name book and looked up.

"Who are you going with?" she asked.

"Rosa."

"You and the spider are going for pizza?"

"Yup. It's kind of a birthday celebration, since no one else seems to be doing much planning around here."

My mum got up, came over and gave me a hug. "Hank, I told you. We've planned a very nice family dinner tomorrow for your birthday."

"I know, Mum," I said. "But Rosa planned this event, and you know how tarantulas are. Once they get something in their mind, they just can't be talked out of it. Don't worry, I'll be back by two."

"Take my mobile phone and call me when you get there," she said. "And no crossing over Broadway. And no talking to strangers. And keep your wallet in your front pocket. And don't forget your house key. And—"

"Mum, I'm just going down the block. Not to Antarctica."

"Right, honey. Just remember to push the number-two key, which is the speed dial for home. I'll be here all morning."

Yeah, picking baby names.

I got up to leave.

"Oh, by the way, Mum. About Digman. It sucks."

CHAPTER 16

TEN OTHER BABY NAMES THAT SUCK MORE THAN DIGMAN

1. Buttcheeks
2. Howie
3. King Mucus the Fifth
4. Madame Lovehandles
5. Stinky
6. Rhino Haunch
7. Puddles
8. Cutie Pie la Rue
9. Hairball La Pew
10. Farty Arty

P.S. I left this list on my mum's pillow before I left. I thought she'd find it helpful.

CHAPTER 17

I WENT INTO MY ROOM and yelled, "It's party time, Rosa!"

She didn't seem as excited as I had hoped. As a matter of fact, she was asleep under a rock. I had the perfect thing to get her excited.

"Hey, look what I made for you," I said, going over to my desk and picking up the bag of party supplies I had bought at the 99-cent store.

I pulled out the smallest party hat ever made, just the right size for a tarantula. I had worked on it the night before. What I did was cut off the very tip of one of the party hats in the packet of six. That tip made a mini cone no bigger than your little fingernail. I even cut the elastic band down to Rosa's size and attached it to either side of the itsy-bitsy hat, being careful not to glue my fingers together like I usually do with superglue.

"Look, Rosa, you've got your own party hat!

How many tarantulas do you know who can say that?"

That did it. She stuck one of her hairy legs out from under the rock, then a second, and so on, until all eight of her gorgeous legs were creeping around her tank. I think she was trying to get a glimpse of her new head wear. She seemed to like it. At least, I think that's what it means when a tarantula's body starts to bounce up and down on all eight legs. Either that or she was hungry for a cricket. But at that moment, I chose to go with the hat theory.

I gathered up the other supplies I had bought for my party. The silver balloon that said "Get Well Soon" was still floating on its string, with plenty of bounce left in it from the day before. I tied it around my wrist, so I could carry it to Harvey's without losing it. I put the party favours, hats and horns into a plastic bag. I had wrapped the whoopee cushion and Rosa's party favour in the comics section from the *New York Post* and a lot of Sellotape. It might seem weird to wrap your own present, but I think a big part of the fun of getting a present is pulling the paper off, and I wanted to be able to do that. Of course, I'd have to help Rosa, but that would be fun, too.

I grabbed the handle on top of her plastic tank and headed for the door.

"Bye, Mum," I hollered as I left the apartment.

As I pushed the lift button, I realized that my left hand or maybe it was my right hand – that's a difference I've never been able to figure out. Anyway, one of my hands was completely empty. I got the key back out of my pocket, opened the door, went in and shouted, "Hello, Mum!" Then I went back to my room, where I had left all the party supplies in the bag on my desk. Welcome to Hank-land, home of the brain that forgets everything except my name.

On the second try, I made it out of the apartment, down the lift and out onto 78th Street. It was really cold, and you could smell that it was going to snow. The wind was coming up my street from the Hudson River, and I had to bend into it to make my way down to Broadway. I didn't want Rosa to get too cold. Even though her legs were pretty hairy, I wasn't sure it was a winter coat. She was from Mexico, after all, and I hear it's hot there. So I unzipped my jacket partway and tucked her small plastic tank inside as far as I could to protect her from the gusts of New York wind.

My first stop was Babka's Bakery, which is three doors down from Harvey's. You're probably thinking that I was going there to get a birthday cake. But surprise! You're wrong! I had changed the cake plan at the last minute. Why not? I was an independent party planner and goer, you know. I could change plans whenever I felt like it.

I pushed open the door and pulled a number from the customer machine that tells you what your place in the queue is. Wow. It was eleven, my favourite number. That was good news already. And even better news was that they were already on number ten, so I only had to wait one minute.

"Who's sick, Hank?" Trudi said. She's worked at Babka's all my life, and my mum and I have bought lots of after-school treats from her.

"No one," I said. "Everyone's fine. Why do you ask?"

"Um ... the balloon," she said, nodding her head at my wrist.

The "Get Well Soon" balloon was so light and floaty that I had forgotten it was tied around my wrist.

"Oh, that!" I said. "No one's sick. No one I know, that is. But I'm sure someone is sick somewhere, so I figured why not send them a get-well wish?"

"That's very sweet of you, Hank," Trudi said. "More people in the world should have your kindness. Now, what can I get for you? No, don't tell me. Your favourite, right?"

"You got it. One black-and-white cookie, which I have been thinking about since seven forty-five this morning."

"Well, you're in luck. They were baked fresh this morning. I'll get you one."

"Make that two," I said to her. "One for now, and one for later."

"Wow. What are you celebrating?"

"As a matter of fact, Trudi, I'm celebrating my birthday."

"Nothing like a black-and-white to do that," she said. "Wait here. I'll go into the back and get you two fresh ones."

While she was gone, the door opened and a woman came in with a pushchair. I didn't even have to turn round to know that she had a buggy, because I heard the little kid screaming and crying all in gibberish.

"Sshhhh, pookie, Mummy's just going to get dessert for dinner, and then we'll go home for a nice nap," she said.

Good plan. It sounded like the kid needed a nice long nap. I turned to catch a glimpse of this Pookie guy. You know exactly what he looked like. Soggy Cheerios plastered on his face, little corduroy trousers that snapped up the inside of his leg. And there was no stopping this kid's wail. Wow, did he have a set of lungs on him.

Then a thought came to me.

Maybe he'd like to meet Rosa. I bet he's never seen a real tarantula. And who's not interested in that?

I reached into my jacket and pulled out Rosa's plastic tank.

"Hey, Pookie. Check this out. Aren't spiders funny?"

I held the plastic tank up in front of him. Wow, I thought Pookie's mum's eyes were going to detach from her head and fly through the glass door without opening it.

"Get that thing away from my baby," she gasped. She was so freaked out, she couldn't even get enough air to speak in a normal voice.

"Rosa's really friendly," I said. "And maybe she could get Pookie there to calm down. Not that he needs to, of course, but if you'd like him to."

"A spider should not be around little children," she said, almost throwing herself in front of Pookie's pram. "It's terrifying!"

"Excuse me," I said in my most polite voice, "but have you noticed something?"

"Yes, I've noticed that you brought a spider into a bakery."

"That's true," I said. "But have you noticed something else? The Pookster there has calmed down. He's stopped crying."

We both turned and looked at the pushchair. Pookie was leaning as far out as he could, trying to get a better look at Rosa. The mum looked totally surprised. And to tell you the truth, I was kind of surprised, too. I thought maybe Rosa would give the baby something to think about other than the soggy Cheerios on his face, but I didn't really think she would work so well. That baby was not only not crying, he was smiling at Rosa. And by the way, there were a few soggy Cheerios stuck to his front four teeth as well.

I felt pretty good about that smile. My idea about Rosa had really worked, and in Hankville, that doesn't happen all that often. I have more bad ideas than good ones. But I'm here to tell you, when I have a good idea and I get to see it

105

in action, it feels pretty good.

"You're excellent with little children," Pookie's mum said to me. "You must have a baby brother or sister."

"Not yet," I said, "but one's coming soon."

"Well, when that baby comes, he or she is going to be awfully lucky to have you as a big brother," she said.

Score one for the Hankster.

Put that compliment on top of the two piping hot, right-out-of-the-oven black-and-white cookies that Trudi had just brought out, and this was turning into a pretty tasty way to start the day.

CHAPTER 18

WHEN I PUSHED OPEN the door from Babka's and stepped onto Broadway, I held the open bag with the black-and-white cookies close to my nose. The cookies were just out of the oven, and the delicious smells coming out of that bag were more than any normal nose could ever want. The minute the door closed, I reached into the bag and took out the top cookie, lifting it very carefully, so I wouldn't squash the second cookie's icing.

I couldn't wait to sink my teeth into that cookie, so I leaned up against the building to get my balance and peeled the wax paper off the top of the cookie very carefully, so I wouldn't pull any of the icing off with it. There it was in my hands, the King of Cookies, the Emperor of All Desserts. For sure, there was no better way to kick off a birthday party.

Then I had to decide whether to break the cookie in half so that one side was all chocolate and the other was all vanilla. Or I could split it in two the other way so that each half had some chocolate and some vanilla. This is a decision I go through every time I get a black-and-white. This time, I decided to split it right down the middle, half chocolate, half vanilla. I had made up my mind that I'd take a bite of one side, then the other, and let the two flavours mix in my mouth like a blender.

Just as I was putting the chocolate half up to my mouth for the first bite, a shadow crossed in front of me and the cookie was snatched out of my hand.

"Here, let me help you with that," a familiar thick-tongued voice said.

Oh no. There was a cookie monster loose in New York, and his name was Nick McKelty.

"Hey, give that back to me, McKelty. It's mine."

McKelty opened his mouth to show the ground-up cookie crumbs and chocolate icing creating brown saliva that was drooling through the gap in his front teeth.

"Here it is," he said. "Still want some?"

"Why don't you do us both a favour and close your mouth?"

"I love these, don't you?" McKelty said. I could hardly understand him. His words were getting lost in his overstuffed mouth. Fortunately, I knew enough to duck when the crumbs from my cookie came flying out of his mouth like mini missiles.

"Yeah, I love them, which is why I bought them. For me to eat, not you, you gorilla."

He reached out to grab the vanilla half, but I was too quick for him. I jumped back and held the cookie up over my head, just out of his reach. He swiped at it like a dancing bear in the circus.

"Gimme," he repeated.

"No way."

The door to the bakery was flung open, and Trudi stepped outside. She had her jacket on and her scarf wrapped around her neck.

"You still here, Hank?" she said. "I thought you'd be off celebrating your birthday by now."

I winced as Trudi said that. I didn't want McKelty to know that I was giving myself a birthday party. I think you'll agree it's not the kind of thing you want to share with the class bully.

"See you later, Trudi," I said, hoping she'd leave before revealing any more private information. Luckily, she left without saying another word, turning left and heading towards the coffee shop on the opposite corner.

"This your birthday, Zipperbutt?" Big Ears McKelty said. I knew he wouldn't miss a gem like that. "And you're all alone? Figures. You're such a loser."

"I'm definitely not alone."

"I don't see any friends here, except that stupid bug."

"This is Rosa, and she's a tarantula, not a bug. And for your information, she's the guest of honour at my party."

"Well, I can't come, because my dad rented out the entire ice-skating rink at Rockefeller Center for just him and me to have a little hockey game."

There it was, the McKelty Factor at work – truth times a hundred. There was no way McKelty's dad had rented out the ice-skating rink. The only ice-skating McKelty was probably doing that day was on a video hockey arcade game at his dad's bowling alley. (And he probably skates on his ankles, if he can skate at all.)

"That works out perfectly for me, because you're not invited, anyway," I said.

"See you, birthday loser," McKelty said,

swiping the vanilla half of the cookie as he lumbered off. "And thanks for the birthday cake."

Even though I was down to one black-and-white, I was trying really hard to keep a positive attitude about the day. I mean, the whole point of giving yourself a birthday party is to have a good time, isn't it? One cookie is plenty, I told myself, and it will taste even better after I've had my piping hot slice of pepperoni.

"Rosa, don't ever forget what I'm about to tell you," I said to her, giving her tank a little shake to make sure she was paying attention. "Always keep a positive attitude."

I thought I saw her listen for half a second before she turned her backside to me and crawled on top of her rock. I actually had more to say on the subject of keeping a positive attitude, but turning her backside to me was a definite sign that she had heard enough. That was OK with me. A good big brother can give useful advice without launching into a whole parent-style lecture that goes on and on and on ... and on.

I felt pretty proud of myself as I headed down the street to Harvey's.

Was I sulking because my parents were having a new baby?

No, I was not.

Was I kicking up a fuss about my parents ignoring my birthday?

No, I was not.

Was I telling myself this was going to be the worst birthday of my life?

No, I was not.

Was I embarrassed about carrying a silver balloon that said "Get Well Soon" down one of the busiest streets of New York City?

Yes, I was.

Hey, what do you expect? I'm only human.

CHAPTER 19

BEFORE I WENT INTO HARVEY'S, I peeked in the glass window to see if there was anyone I knew inside. I confess, my experience running into Nick McKelty on the street had made me a little uncomfortable. It's one thing to throw yourself a birthday party. It's another thing to do it in front of your classmates.

It's a good thing I checked. Sitting on the front two stools at the counter, right next to the window, were Joelle Atkins and her mum. Joelle Atkins is Nick McKelty's girlfriend, and the thing she loves best in the whole world, other than Nick McKelty, is her mobile phone. I knew that if she saw me with Rosa and my "Get Well Soon" balloon, she'd be on the phone to everyone we know, giving them the full scoop on my party-for-one.

That's OK. I could wait. It wasn't even eleven o'clock yet, so I had lots of time before the lunch rush at Harvey's.

I leaned up against the beige concrete building and just watched the people hurrying by on the pavement. It was cold and I could feel my nose starting to turn red. To pass the time, I decided to count all the people who were wearing scarves. I quit when I got to forty-three. Or maybe it was thirty-four. There were too many of them going by too fast, and the numbers were starting to get all jumbled up in my head. So I decided to count all the people who were wearing sunglasses instead.

I quit that game when I was still at zero, fifteen minutes after I started. It turns out not too many people wear sunglasses when it's February in New York City and it's grey and cloudy outside. I guess there's no surprise there.

Oops. There was one person wearing sunglasses, and she was looking right at me. It was Joelle Atkins, staring me down, almost nose-to-nose.

That's what happens when you daydream, folks. The Joelle Atkinses of the world stick their noses in your face when you least suspect it.

"Tell me that's not a spider," she barked. She sounded like a yappy, bad-tempered little dog. "Because if it is, I'm going to scream."

"Then scream away," I said, "because you're about to meet my pet baby tarantula, up close and personal."

I held Rosa's tank up to Joelle's face. Rosa took one look at Joelle's crabby, mean expression and instantly started flicking stomach hairs at her.

"Aaaagggggghhhhhhhhhhh!" Joelle shrieked. It was loud, and I mean screechy, ear-splitting, spine-tingling loud. I heard taxis slamming on their brakes all up and down the street. It was pretty funny to see Joelle take off down Broadway, like a wild cheetah was chasing her.

"Young man," her mother said, turning to me with a nasty look on her face. "There should be a law against taking a spider for a walk." Then she bent down to pick up the phone Joelle had let slip out of her hand when she took off.

"Here, honey, you dropped your mobile phone," she called after Joelle.

As her mother reached her, Joelle grabbed the phone and started dialling with all ten fingers. She was probably calling the tarantula police.

"Good work on the hair flicking, Rosa," I said to her. "But now we're going into Harvey's, so I'm going to need to see your restaurant manners."

Rosa flicked a single stomach hair at me.

"No, that is not OK, Rosa. I need your co-operation, and I need it now."

I stared at her, but she looked away, hanging onto the side of the tank and pulsating up and down. I took that as a sign she was blowing me off.

"Rosa, if you don't behave, I'm going to have to take you home and you'll lose your going-out privileges. I don't want to do that, but if you force me, I will."

Hank Zipzer, did you hear yourself? You just sounded like your dad.

Wow, that was a shock. Did being a big brother mean I was going to turn into my father? Was I suddenly going to start talking about losing television privileges and never running with a toothpick in your mouth and clearing your own plate after dinner? Oh, boy. I made a mental note to pull back on the Stanley Zipzerisms.

I opened the door and went into Harvey's.

There are only three tables in Harvey's and exactly twelve seats at the counter. I know this because I've sat in every one of them, enjoying the perfect slice of pepperoni pizza with extra cheese. Harvey knows exactly what I want, so I never have to order when I am there. I look at him, he looks at me, and says, "The usual for the kid." Before you know it, Miguel, the cook, delivers me a piping hot slice on a double paper plate with a pink lemonade on the side.

Harvey was behind the counter wearing his usual white apron over his white shirt with his name embroidered over the pocket.

You can tell that Harvey likes all of the food he makes because his apron only fits halfway around him. His stomach looks like he swallowed five basketballs. He wears a mini chef's hat on his head, which doesn't completely cover his very neat black hair that never moves. He must use lots and lots of hair cream to keep it like that. It's like he's wearing a white hat on top of a black hat.

"Hey, kid," Harvey said. "Just get your hair cut?"

"No, why do you ask?"

"You got a balloon there. Don't you get one after every haircut?"

"Yeah, but this is my birthday balloon. I couldn't think of any other place I'd rather celebrate than right here."

"Great," Harvey said, taking out a wet cloth and starting to wipe down the counter space in front of me. "How many places do you need...? I'll set them up special for you."

"Just one," I answered. "Well, make that one and a half."

"That bony little pal of yours coming in?"

"You mean Robert?" I said, laughing almost to the point of snorting. "No, he's probably at the library studying the fact that animals that lay eggs don't have belly buttons."

"Last time he was in here he asked me if I knew that a shrimp's heart was in its head," Harvey said.

"That sounds like Robert, all right. His head is full of that kind of stuff, and you know he's not too shy to share it."

"I'll remember that. So if it's not the brainiac, who's the half?"

I lifted Rosa's little tank and held it up so Harvey could see her.

"You're having a birthday party with that thing?" Harvey didn't look too happy to see Rosa.

"That thing is my baby sister substitute, Rosa. And she's the guest of honour."

"She's locked up in there, right?"

"Absolutely, Harvey. Tight as a drum."

"Well, ordinarily, I don't allow web-spinning

things in here, but since it's your birthday party and I don't want to be a party pooper, I'll make an exception this time." He leaned up close to me and whispered, "Could you do me a favour, though, and sit at the last stool at the counter, so you don't upset the other customers?"

Actually, that turned out to be a fine suggestion, because it gave me room to tie my balloon under the seat of my stool and to set up the wrapped party favours between me and the jukebox on the counter. After they were set up, I reached into the plastic bag and pulled out the two hats and horns, one for me and one for Rosa.

I put my hat on and sat there staring at Rosa, trying to figure out exactly how a person straps a party hat on a tarantula. Somehow, I didn't think she'd like the idea of having a rubber band under her belly. And then it hit me. I pulled the elastic band as far as it would go and slid it around the plastic tank, so the hat was resting right on top of the lid.

I noticed that the man next to me had put down his meatball sub sandwich that was dripping with tomato sauce and was watching what I was doing.

"I didn't think the spider would be comfortable in an elastic chinstrap," I explained.

"That's very inventive," he said.

I wasn't exactly sure what "inventive" meant, but I was pretty sure it was a compliment, and that made me feel really good. So I said "Thank you" on instinct. He nodded, so I assumed I had guessed correctly.

While I was waiting for my pizza, the place started to fill up. When I came in, only one table had people at it, but by the time Harvey slid my slice in front of me, all three tables were full, and so were at least half the seats at the counter.

"Here you go, kid," Harvey said, sliding the double paper plates in front of me. "Since it's your birthday, consider this on the house."

"Thanks, Harvey."

As much as I wanted to take a bite, I knew I had to let the pizza cool for a minute so I wouldn't burn the roof of my mouth. While I was waiting, I took a second to look at what I had created.

There I was, with a birthday hat on, a great party favour waiting to be opened, a balloon flapping in the breeze every time someone opened the front door, and a new family member enjoying the day with me.

Hank Zipzer, you know how to throw a party! As a matter of fact, you could open a business doing this. I could see it before me. My business cards would read, "Hank Zipzer, Party Planner Extraordinaire." Except I don't have a clue how to spell "extraordinaire", so maybe the cards could say, "Hank Zipzer, Party Planner Who's Really Good."

I was almost finished with my pizza slice when I realized that I was being rude. I mean, here was Rosa, smelling the fabulous combination of pepperoni and cheese and toasty crust aromas that were drifting into the airholes of her tank. She was obviously hungry, because she was running in circles in her tank, up and down the sides and across the top. She was definitely dying for a taste, and I hadn't offered her even so much as a crumb.

"OK, Rosa," I whispered to her. "It's your turn now."

I tore off a piece of my pizza, about the size of my thumbnail. I made sure that I got crust, cheese and pepperoni on the tiny bite. My plan was to slide the lid off just enough to drop the piece of pizza in, then close it really fast and lock it back up again.

But plans don't always work out like they do in your mind.

CHAPTER 20

HERE'S A FACT that I know about tarantulas even without Robert telling me. They are fast. Let me repeat that word. Faaassssstttttt!

Before I had slid the top open half an inch, Rosa was up and over the side and on the counter, barrelling towards the man with the sloppy meatball sandwich. When he got a look at her running towards him, he jumped off his stool backwards and backed up so fast, he sat down in the lap of the lady sitting at the table behind him.

"Oh my word!" screamed the lady. "I don't believe we've even met!"

Rosa didn't stop at the meatball sandwich. Oh no. She was up and over it like it was a small hill. As she scurried down the lime green counter, she left red tomato sauce tracks where her eight legs were running towards a really pretty teenage girl who was eating a bowl of minestrone soup. Barrelling along the countertop, it looked like Rosa was leaving coloured footprints in wet cement. And then suddenly, she was gone – disappeared into the bowl of soup.

"Eeuuuwwwwww!" the girl screamed. "Gross! There's a hairy thing splashing around in my soup!"

Harvey's head spun round just in time to see Rosa swimming the breaststroke across the bowl of minestrone.

"Hey, kid," he yelled to me. "You promised to keep that thing under control!"

That snapped me into action. I got up and dashed over to the stool where the girl had been sitting. I stuck my hand into the soup, grabbing for Rosa. But as I've already pointed out, tarantulas are fast. All I came up with was a fistful of courgette and some soggy cabbage.

"Rosa!" I yelled. "Get back here this instant. This is completely unacceptable behaviour."

She was in no mood to listen to instructions. She stood just out of my reach on the counter, pulsating, pumping up and down on her eight legs like she was on a bouncing trampoline.

"I need your co-operation now!" I said. "Remember what we said about using our restaurant manners."

I extended my hand towards her. Slowly. Slowly. Just as I went for the grab, she took off the other way, running all the way to the other end of the counter where Harvey keeps his coconut cake under a glass domed dish. Everybody from that end of the restaurant was on their feet now, and they weren't happy.

"A spider!" yelled a woman in a green knit cap.

"I'm allergic to bugs!" called a man in a bow tie. "They give me a rash on my elbows!"

"*Mamma mia!*" cried an Italian woman with a small mustache. "It's going to bite us, one by one."

"Hank, please!" yelled Harvey. "Capture that thing."

"I'm trying, Harvey! I really am! But babies have a mind of their own."

Rosa looked over at Harvey and moved in closer, close enough for him to try to bonk her with his wooden spoon. She reached her hind leg up to her tummy and flicked a few choice tarantula hairs in his direction.

"Eeeuuuwww!" the teenage girl called. "The beast is flicking hair all over the place. Gross!"

That made Harvey jump back, landing on

his butt on the sandwich counter. His butt hit a bull's-eye on the squeeze bottle of yellow mustard, which squirted all over his rear end. You can only imagine what it looked like all over the back of his trousers. Let me just say, it didn't look like mustard.

Everyone took off to the back of the restaurant and stood huddled in a corner, smooshed into a ball of people. Rosa must have seen them and thought to herself, *Hey, this is fun.* She made another dash down the counter towards them, and just before she got to the very end, she jumped onto the last stool in front of them. They ran screaming with their hands in the air, into the opposite corner by the window. The man in the bow tie, who had dropped his pizza slice, stepped on it and went sliding on the cheese along the linoleum floor. He looked like he was skateboarding.

"Whooaaaa!" he yelled.

"Nice moves, dude," a skateboarder from one of the other tables called out.

A part of me wanted to step back and enjoy the scene. I mean, let's face it. It was pretty funny. A guy in a bow tie skateboarding on melted cheese? Come on. You have to laugh. Besides, we all know that Rosa is basically harmless.

But the other part of me, the big brother part, knew that I had to be responsible and handle the situation quickly. That part of me knew that this was not a laughing matter.

And that was the part that cleared my brain and instantly created a plan of attack. I raced down to the end of the counter and took the glass dome top off the coconut cake plate. I crept as quickly and silently as I could behind Rosa and in a swift (and if I say so myself) precise move, captured her under the top. All the customers broke into applause. I didn't realize until that moment that I had been holding my breath, which I let out in a big sigh.

I gave Rosa a stern look.

"You and I have to talk, young lady," I said. "You can bet there will be consequences for this."

Holy moly! Now I wasn't just sounding like my father, I had turned into him!

I turned to all the customers and tried to smile, like this was no big deal.

"It's OK, folks," I said. "The situation is under control, and there is no danger. Please go back to enjoying your meal."

"What about my soup?" the teenage girl said.

"It's probably got spider pee in it."

"Rosa and I would like to buy you another bowl," I said, without hesitating.

I reached into my jeans pocket to see how much money I had. I couldn't count it very well, so I just laid it all down on the counter, pretending I knew what I was doing with it.

"This should cover it," Harvey said, taking a dollar and some change. I had no idea how much I had left, but I picked it all up and put it in my pocket with great confidence. You learn to put on a brave face when you can't do maths in your head.

"Now, Hank, since you're finished with your pizza, I think it's time to take your spider home," Harvey said. "And by the way, make sure you leave her there next time you come in for a slice."

As I was gathering up my things, the front door opened and in came Papa Pete.

"Hey, Hankie," he said. "I stopped by the apartment and your mum said you were here."

"Papa Pete, I've never been so happy to see you."

"We had a little excitement here," Harvey said. "The kid will tell you about it. Right after he escorts the spider out of here ... which he will be doing immediately if not sooner."

I looked at Rosa sitting under the glass cake dome and Papa Pete followed my gaze. There she was, having her own party under there, happy as can be. She had found a shred of coconut and was having a grand old time lapping it up, or whatever spiders do with birthday cake.

"Hank, what's she doing here?" Papa Pete asked.

"I invited her to my birthday party," I said. "But she hogged the show, just like a typical baby. That's what you get for trying to share. The baby takes over."

"Families share," Papa Pete said. "That's what they do. With certain exceptions. And one of them is birthdays. That's your special day. No sharing required."

"Tell that to Rosa," I said.

"I will, as soon as we get her out of Harvey's cake dish. She seems to have made herself at home with the coconut frosting."

I went and got Rosa's plastic tank, tore off another little piece of pizza and dropped it in. I brought it down to the cake dome and quickly lifted it just enough to slide Rosa's tank inside. She didn't attempt to get out this time, because she was busy chowing down on her dessert. But within a few seconds, the pizza smell hit her, and she stopped eating the coconut and made a bee-line for the pizza. Who wouldn't? Harvey's pizza is the best.

Once she was inside her tank, Papa Pete lifted the cake dome and I slammed on the lid.

"Mission accomplished," Papa Pete said.

I gathered my party favours and balloon, thanked Harvey for his patience, waved good-bye to all the other customers and headed out the door.

I had the feeling they were all very happy to see us go.

HAPTER 21

As Papa Pete walked me home, I thought about everything that had happened on my party day. And if I give myself any more parties in the future, here are ten rules I made for myself.

HANK ZIPZER'S TEN RULES
FOR SELF-PARTY GIVING

1. Only invite two-legged creatures with nostrils. (Except for Cheerio, who is used to parties and has great party manners.)
2. Eat your black-and-white birthday cookie first in case one of your guests decides to take a bath in a bowl of soup.
3. Don't forget to take your whoopee cushion party favour or you won't be able to put it under the big bum of Nick McKelty.
4. Make sure your balloon doesn't say "Get Well Soon" because all the grown-ups will

want to check and make sure you don't have a fever.

5. Take at least one bite of your pepperoni pizza, and if a spider gets loose before you have time to finish it, make sure that you ask for a doggie bag. When you get home, remind the dog that doggie bags are for people.

6. I was just starting to think up Number Six when we reached the front door of my building. Sorry that I didn't get to ten. I would have, if the walk from Harvey's to my apartment wasn't so short.

CHAPTER 22

Papa Pete dropped me off in front of my building, and as I got in the elevator, my fingers were itching to press the six button instead of ten. Six is Frankie's floor, and I really wanted to check in with him and tell him the story of The Spider Who Ate My Birthday Party. When you have a best friend, there's nothing better than being able to share a great adventure, even if it turned your birthday party into a bad horror movie.

I didn't press six, though. I had made such a big deal about giving myself my own birthday party and not needing any of my friends to be there that I felt I should finish the day out all by myself. I mean, either you're an independent party giver and goer, or you're not. Right? And that's same reason I didn't push the fourth-floor button, which is Ashley's floor. So my thumb had no choice but to find its way to the tenth-floor button, which would take me home.

"Rosa, I hope you're thinking about what you just did," I said to her as we rode up the elevator. "I really had a great party planned, and it did not include you doing the backstroke in a bowl of minestrone."

Rosa just sat there, hanging on the side of her tank, pulsating. But her body was turned away from me. I don't think she could look me square in the eye. She knew. I truly believed she had learned her lesson. And I didn't want to punish her. After all, she's just a baby.

"Hey, everyone, I'm home," I called as I walked in the door. Silence yelled back at me. The only thing that broke the silence was Cheerio, who scampered down the hallway and, as he always does, slid the last seven feet on the slippery floor.

"Hey, boy," I said, scratching him behind the ears. "At least someone's glad to see me."

I decided to put Rosa's tank down on the coffee table in the living room, so she could have a.look around and get used to that room, since she hadn't spent a lot of time in there. Then I went into my bedroom and tossed my jacket on my bed instead of hanging it up right away. I made a mental note to hang it up before my mum saw it. I looked around for Cheerio, who usually follows me wherever I go, so that I could have a friendly boy-dog wrestle, which is our tradition when I come home. He wasn't there, but I heard him growling in the living room ... a low growl that came from the bottom of his throat. This was definitely not a Cheerio sound.

I raced into the living room and found him standing on the coffee table, crouching like a lion and inching himself towards Rosa's tank. He had his head down and his eyes never left Rosa's tank. He was definitely giving her the evil eye. Wow, my little Cheerio suddenly looked like one of those hunting dogs that you see on Animal Planet.

Rosa wasn't taking it too well. She was hunched in the corner of her tank, hanging upside down off the upper corner next to the lid. She had made herself into the smallest ball possible. Seven of her legs were wrapped around her body, and she was using the eighth to hang on for dear life. I could tell she was trying to make herself invisible, and I couldn't blame her. I mean, to her, Cheerio must have looked like a T. Rex about to gobble her up for lunch.

"Cheerio!" I said in a voice so harsh it surprised even me. "This is completely unacceptable. Get off the table this instant."

Cheerio looked at me and growled.

"Don't use that tone of growl with me, young man," I said. "And get off that table immediately. You're scaring your baby sister. You should be nice to her."

Cheerio only did half of what I commanded him to do. He did jump down off the table, but instead of being nice to Rosa, he started to run in circles around the table. He usually chases his tail around in circles, which is his hobby, but now, it seemed like he was running in circles to keep me from getting close to the table.

"Cheerio, sit!" I said. "And I'm not kidding."

I must have had that "you better listen and listen now" tone to my voice that my dad is so good at, because Cheerio's bottom hit the floor at lightning speed. The truth is, and I don't mean to insult Cheerio, when you're a dachshund with those short legs, you don't have far to go before your butt is introduced to the floor.

"That's more like it," I said to him. Then I reached out and grabbed Rosa's tank. She was still curled up in the top corner, although the motion of me lifting the tank made her sway from side to side like she was on a swing.

"You OK, girl?" I said to her. "Cheerio didn't mean to scare you. He's probably just jealous of you, because you came to the party and he wasn't invited. It's hard to have a new baby in the house."

Whoa, suddenly it hit me like a sack of cat's-eye marbles. Cheerio had the same feelings that I was experiencing. I mean, he had always been the main dog in our house, and my favourite pet. We had a special relationship, him and me, like Batman and Robin. Now that Rosa was here, he was scared that he was going to lose his place with me.

Wow, did I know that feeling.

I put Rosa down behind me, out of Cheerio's sight. Then I kneeled down right in front of him and scratched him on his favourite spot. I started at his ears and worked my way down the sides of his mouth, ending up at his nose. I could tell that this was a super deluxe scratch treatment for him because he got a faraway look in his eyes, and his back leg – do not ask me which one, because I don't know if it was his right or his left – started to scratch the air like it does when he's over-the-moon happy.

"Don't worry, Cheerio," I said. "I still love you and I always will."

Cheerio put his head in my lap and made a sound that I swear sounded like, "I'm sorry, Rosa."

CHAPTER 23

SEVEN THINGS THAT HAPPENED THAT AFTERNOON THAT ARE KIND OF BORING (OK, VERY BORING) SO YOU MIGHT WANT TO SKIP THIS LIST

The rest of that day was, well, let's just say regular. I mean, after a birthday party where your pet tarantula chases a crowd of people around your favourite pizza parlour, you have to admit that an average afternoon is not going to seem all that exciting. But I promised you a list, so here it is.

1. I hung up my jacket. I'm not going to tell you in which cupboard because then you'd be so bored, you'd close this book and never pick it up again, which I don't want you to do because there are exciting things coming.

2. My mum helped me work on a report about Why Tugboats Are Known as the Weight Lifters of the Sea. I won't tell you why they are, because ... well ... see Number One above.
3. My dad watched *Jeopardy!* and got in a bad mood because he missed the Double Jeopardy question where you had to name a small town at the base of the Matterhorn Mountain in Switzerland. (In case you're wondering, the town is called Zermat, a boring but true fact.)
4. Emily cleaned Katherine's cage and insisted on putting the dirty newspapers in my wastebasket instead of hers, which stinks up my room for a week.
5. We had garlic tofu burgers for dinner, which stinks up the kitchen for a week.
6. I went to bed hungry.
7. I fell fast asleep, but here's where I'm going to end this boring list because what happened next was not boring in the least. Read on. I know you, and I'm sure you're going to find it very exciting.

CHAPTER 24

WHEN I WENT TO SLEEP THAT NIGHT, I had the best dream of all time. It was so real that I swear I thought I could reach out and touch it.

I couldn't have been asleep for more than three minutes when a giant baby came floating in through my window and pushed on my cheek with its finger to wake me up. But this was no regular giant baby, no sir. He was so tall, his head bumped against the ceiling of my room as he floated over to me. He was as big around as a blimp, and he seemed to be made of giant, squashy, white marshmallows. All he was wearing was a nappy and a gigantic smile.

"Hankie, come with me," the humongous baby said, holding out his roly-poly marshmallow hand.

It seems weird now, but in my dream I wasn't scared at all. I just put my hand in his, which felt soft and sticky. He pulled me over to my window and pointed to the lights of New York City below.

"We go there," he said.

"Whoa, big baby," I answered. "Some of us humans don't fly. And I'm one of them."

"You safe, Hankie. Come now."

And without even deciding to go out of the window, suddenly I was floating, hand in hand with the baby, over the west side of New York. It was so beautiful from up there. I felt light as a feather and powerful as Superman all at the same time. I was laughing so hard that I almost let go of his hand, but luckily I couldn't because it was so marshmallow-sticky.

Suddenly, the big baby swooped down from the sky. It felt like we were on one of those very fast lifts that shoots down from the 44th floor of a skyscraper. Your body is on the ground floor, but your stomach is still on the 44th. It took a minute for me to get my stomach out of my mouth and push it back down where it belonged.

The baby was pointing to something below.

"Hankie, look!"

We were hovering over 79th Street, where there is a big hill that takes you down to

Riverside Park and the Hudson River beyond. The wind comes up off the river, and during the winter, that wind is icy cold. But it didn't seem to bother us. Here I was, flying around in my Mets pyjamas in the middle of winter, and I was as warm as a cup of hot cocoa with a spoonful of whipped cream.

I looked at where the baby was pointing, and my heart started to beat really fast. I don't know why, but I could feel that something terrible was about to happen. A dad was pushing a buggy down 79th Street towards the park. I heard a little song in the distance, and then I realized it was his mobile phone ringing. He let go of the pushchair for a split second to answer his phone. In that instant, the wind came up and pushed the pram down the hill. It took off as if it were a racing car coming down the straightaway.

"Hey, Mister," I yelled. "Get off the phone. Your baby's flying like a rocket down the hill."

The man continued chatting on the phone and didn't even notice that the carriage had got away from him and was heading down 79th Street, picking up speed as it went along. I kept trying to alert him, but no matter how loud I yelled, the man still didn't hear me.

"Marshmallow Baby," I said. "He's not listening!"

"Only Marshmallow Baby can hear you," he said to me.

I looked down again, and what I saw made my heart beat like a drum. A delivery truck filled with fruits and vegetables was making its way along West End Avenue. It looked to me like it was going to reach 79th Street just at the same time the baby's pram was going to shoot off the kerb. I didn't even want to think about what would happen next!

"We have to save the baby!" I yelled.

"I not want to," the Marshamallow Baby giggled. "I sleepy."

"You better wake up, and wake up now," I said to the baby. "We have work to do. Let's go and take care of business."

The baby looked at me and wrinkled up his pudgy nose.

"I mean it," I said to him. "I'm older than you, and I know what I'm talking about."

I must have sounded like a guy in charge, because with that, Marshmallow Baby swooped down towards the out-of-control pushchair. It felt like we were speeding down the steepest part of a roller coaster.

We had wasted so much time that I wasn't sure if we were going to reach the pushchair in time, even though we were going at breakneck speed. It was quite a chase. As we finally pulled alongside the carriage, I looked inside and saw a little girl with a pink bonnet whose eyes were wide open in terror.

"Have no fear, the Hankster is here!" I called to her.

The little baby just looked at me. She was too scared even to cry.

"Marshmallow Baby," I yelled. "Get me as close to the buggy as you can!"

Marshmallow Baby extended his arm as far as he could, which brought me next to the speeding pushchair.

"Now hold on to my hand as tight as you can," I called to him, "because I'm going to try something. Whatever you do, don't let go!"

Marshmallow Baby grabbed on tight to my hand. While he was holding on to me, I reached out as far as I could, straining to grab hold of the handle just before it reached the bottom of the street, where it was heading for the delivery truck. I stretched out until I thought my body was going to snap like a wishbone. The very tips of my fingers finally made contact with the handle of the pushchair, but I couldn't really grab on to it.

"Marshmallow Baby," I called. "I need another inch. You're made of marshmallows, so try to stretch as far as you can. Think elastic. Think gooey. Think longer."

To my amazement, the baby's hand began to stretch way out, like when you take chewed bubble gum out of your mouth and pull it into a long, pink string. That allowed me to get close enough so I could get my hand completely around the handle of the pushchair. I pulled with all my might and at the same time Marshmallow Baby stopped in mid-air, as if he had stepped on a magical brake. The buggy came to a halt just before it reached the street.

Whoa! That was close.

I looked up and saw the fruit and vegetable truck whizz by so fast that I could feel the air whoosh behind it and the heat from its tailpipe.

"Don't worry, little girl," I said to the baby in the pushchair. "You're safe now."

The dad came running up, completely out of breath.

"I'm so grateful to you!" he said. "I don't know how to thank you."

"No thanks necessary," I told him. "I really like helping babies out. Don't you feel the same way, M.B.?"

"It feel good," Marshmallow Baby laughed.

And before the man could say another word, we had shot back up into the night sky, leaving a white flash of marshmallow goop trailing behind us. We were heading across town, flying over the Museum of Natural History.

"Hey, M.B.," I said. "Have you ever seen the gigantic whale hanging from the ceiling in there?"

"Me scared of it," M.B. said.

"There's nothing to be scared of," I reassured him. "It's not real. Besides, whales are very nice creatures. They're mammals, you know."

Wow, look at me.

I was teaching this guy science facts. I don't know much about animals and things, certainly not nearly as much as my sister, Emily, or her nerdling boyfriend, Robert, but I knew a whole lot more than this baby. That felt pretty good. Hank Zipzer, science teacher. At your service.

We flew over Central Park, banking left (or maybe it was right) over the boathouse that sits by the side of Central Park Lake. Looking down, I saw a boy about my age, who was putting his baby brother, or maybe it was a sister – I couldn't tell – into a rowboat. Silvery moonbeams were streaking across the water. They lit up the baby like a ... well ... like a moonbeam. The boy was about to set foot in the boat and had just untied it from the dock. What a nice big brother, I thought to myself. Taking the new baby for a rowboat ride around Central Park Lake.

Suddenly, from out of nowhere, a glowing green Frisbee shot across the park and landed on the dock right next to the rowboat. I know this sounds weird, but hey, it's my dream and I'm telling it just the way it happened in my brain.

Anyway, this Frisbee landed on the dock and the boy jogged over to pick it up. While his back was turned, the rowboat started to drift away from the dock and towards the centre of the lake. The baby screamed, holding its little arms out for its big brother.

Wow, I wonder if our new baby will hold its arms out for me?

Marshmallow Baby and I saw this happening

at exactly the same time. I looked over at him and said, "You know what to do, M.B."

He swooped down to the lake and got behind the boat, but I couldn't reach it. This time, I held on to M.B.'s nappy to give me the most stretch room. Reaching out as far as I could, I was able to grab the boat and give it a gentle shove towards the dock. Slowly, the baby drifted back to its big brother, who grabbed the rope and quickly tied it up onto the dock. The big brother reached out and picked up his baby brother. When he turned around, I was astonished to see that he looked just like me.

"Hank! Hank!"

Was that my mother's voice? What was she doing in my dream?

"Hank! Wake up!" the voice called again.

I opened my eyes and there was my mum, sitting on the edge of my bed, smiling down at me.

"What were you dreaming about, birthday boy?"

"Babies," I said.

"Oh. Was it a good or bad dream?"

"Surprisingly enough, Mum, it was a great dream."

"So you think maybe you're getting used to the idea of a new baby in the house?"

I thought about her question for a long time before I answered.

"You know, Mum," I said at last, "I think there's a lot that baby is going to need me for."

"I agree, sweetie," she said. "You're going to be a fabulous big brother."

"Like what if the baby is speeding down a hill towards the Hudson River in a runaway pushchair? I could stop it before it ran into traffic."

My mum laughed and tousled my hair.

"I don't think that's going to happen, Hank."

"You never know, Mum. You never know."

"Why don't you get dressed, honey. We have a little birthday surprise for you."

"I know," I said. "We already discussed this. The quiet family day at home, followed by the quiet family dinner ... at home."

"Just get dressed," she said. "And by the way, make sure you pick out a clean T-shirt."

I had no idea why it mattered so much that I had to have a clean T-shirt to walk from my bedroom to our living room for a quiet family day. But mums are mums, and they like you to do what they say. So I did.

CHAPTER 25

WHEN I GOT TO THE LIVING ROOM, no one was even there. I walked into the kitchen, and there was no breakfast cooking. Man, they had said this was going to be a quiet day, but this was ridiculous. Where was everyone?

Pretty soon, my dad came into the kitchen with my Mets sweatshirt and my coat.

"Here, Hank, put these on," he said.

"Hey, Dad, isn't this kind of overdressing for a quiet day at home?" I said.

"There's been a change of plans. We're going for a walk."

"Your father and I decided that a walk would build up a nice appetite for dinner later," my mum said, coming into the kitchen and pulling on her furry red coat.

"It's a scientific fact that exercise stimulates the appetite," Emily chimed in as she came in, carrying her pink parka with a giraffe on it that she got at the Bronx Zoo.

A walk wasn't exactly what I had in mind, but when the Zipzer family is going forward, there is no way of reversing its direction. So I put on my Mets sweatshirt and coat and we left the apartment.

My dad led the walk, setting a brisk pace up Amsterdam Avenue.

"What's the rush?" I asked him, taking big steps just trying to keep up with him.

"No rush," he said, walking even faster.

"You're father's just excited," my mum said. Wow, it must be really dull to be a grown-up, if going for a walk down Amsterdam Avenue is something that gets them all excited.

When we had walked about seven blocks, my dad started to slow down right in front of the entrance to McKelty's Roll 'N' Bowl.

"How about if we stick our heads in for a minute?" my dad said.

"Good idea," my mum said, sounding a little weird. "Papa Pete might be practicing."

"He never bowls on Sunday morning," I said. "He rests his bowling fingers on Sundays."

"Let's take a look, anyway," Emily said. "You never know."

My family was definitely acting strangely, but then, the Zipzer family can be that way some of the time. OK, most of the time.

We walked up the stairs, and my dad held the door to the bowling alley open for me.

"You go first, Hank," he said. "See if Papa Pete is in there."

I walked in and looked around. The bowling alley seemed dark, and very quiet. The usual sounds of balls rolling down the polished wooden alleys and people yelling about their gutter balls were completely missing.

"Hello!" I called out. "Anyone here?"

Suddenly, the lights went on and a crowd of familiar faces jumped out from behind the shoe desk and the bowling ball racks and the video games. Everyone I knew was there. Papa Pete and Frankie and Ashley and their parents and Heather Payne and Ryan Shimozato from school, and my Aunt Maxine and Uncle Gary and their maniac twins. Even Mrs Fink was there – she had her false teeth in, uppers and lowers! Wow, this really must be a big occasion.

"SURPRISE!" everyone yelled at once. "HAPPY BIRTHDAY, HANK!"

I turned around to look at my family. They

were all smiling and clapping and even Emily was jumping up and down.

"You got me!" I said to them. "Wow! Wowee wow wow. Did you ever get me!"

"Happy birthday, honey," my mum said, giving me a big kiss on the cheek. I was so overwhelmed by the surprise that I didn't even care that she'd kissed me in public.

"Your mother has been planning this surprise party for weeks," my dad said.

"I helped, too," Emily said. "I made the party favours."

OK, so the party favours were little handmade books called *101 Fascinating Facts about Reptiles, written and illustrated by Emily Grace Zipzer.* But trust me, I didn't care. Those party favours were the only lame part of the party and, hey, it's the thought that counts. The rest of the day couldn't have been more fantastic.

It was the greatest Surprise Birthday Bowling Brunch Party anyone could want. We had bowling and root-beer floats and present opening and video-game playing. The only thing that would have made it more perfect would have been if we had played pin the tail on the donkey and the donkey was Nick McKelty.

I was totally one hundred per cent surprised.

Oh yeah, and I was totally one hundred per cent happy, too.

Frankie and Ashley told me that they got a huge kick out of the fact that they were able to keep such a great party a secret. Turns out they had never planned to go shopping in New Jersey for the new baby. And they had spent all day Saturday setting up the decorations for the party. They made it a magic theme, with top hats and magic wands for decorations and a black cape for the tablecloth.

Everyone brought presents and their good-time party attitudes, even Robert, who did find it necessary to point out that the birthday cake was invented by the ancient Greeks, who baked it in the shape of the full moon in honour of their moon goddess, Artemis. Everyone stood there for a moment in silence, wondering if my mother had baked a cake that tasted like moon rocks. Luckily, Robert's fact was not a total party killer, because right after that, Papa Pete challenged me to a bowl-off.

Everyone cheered for me and stomped their feet when I won. Hey, it was my birthday. I have a feeling Papa Pete let me win, which is what grandfathers do on your special day.

When the cake and bowling and presents were over, I stood up to make a little speech. I told everyone how happy I was, what a great birthday I'd had, and I thanked my parents for giving me such a special celebration. And then, to my total surprise, this came out of my mouth.

"Next year at this time, there will be one more Zipzer at my birthday party. And you know what? That is just fine with me."

CHAPTER 26

TEN THINGS THAT ARE
BETTER THAN HAVING A SURPRISE
BOWLING BIRTHDAY BRUNCH

1. Nothing.

An interview with Henry Winkler

What's your favourite thing about Hank Zipzer?

My favourite thing about Hank Zipzer is that he is resourceful. Just because he can't figure something out doesn't mean that he won't find a way.

I love his sense of humour. Even though Lin and I write the books together, when we meet in the morning to work we never know where the characters or the story will take us. Hank and his friends make us laugh all the time.

What was it like growing up with dyslexia?

When I was growing up in New York City, no one knew what dyslexia was. I was called stupid and lazy, and I was told that I was not living up to my potential. It was, without a doubt, painful.

I spent most of my time covering up the fact

that reading, writing, spelling, maths, science – actually, every subject but lunch – was really, really difficult for me. If I went to the shop and paid the bill with paper money and I was given coins back for change, I had no idea how to count up the change in my head. I just trusted that everyone was being honest.

What's it like working as a team to write the World's Greatest Underachiever books?

We have the most wonderful time working together. Lin sits at the computer, and I walk in a circle in front of her desk. If I start talking like the characters, Lin kindly types it in because I don't use a computer. Or, she'll tell me to stop for minute because she's got a great idea and her fingers fly across the keyboard. Sometimes, I'll write my chapters in long hand and Lin will transcribe them and correct my spelling. When the book is done, we both go over it to see if we've left anything out, or perhaps we'll find a better joke for one of the characters or better action in a scene. When it's completely done, we send it to our editor, and she sends back her notes that we then incorporate.

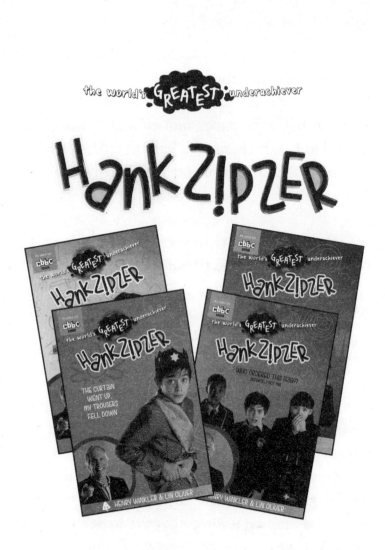

Love the TV series?
Read the books!